WHAT REVIEWERS ARE SAYING ...

ABOUT *ENSNARED BY INNOCENCE*

**"Witty, Enchanting and Roaring Hot!
I think I've found a new author to binge!** I would definitely recommend it as a good gateway book to shape-shifters or to lovers of historical romance." 5-Star Goodreads Review

"I would give this a 10/10 rating. **Beautifully written by a very talented author... PLEASE read this brilliant novel.** I cannot wait for the next in series." 5-Star BookBub Review

"Fantastic Story!! I really enjoyed this book!" 5-Star Reviewer Emily P.

Thanks to my phenomenal proofreader Judy for her quality work, her fun and timely emails and especially for putting up with my repeated need to reschedule.

If only these stories could go straight from my brain and onto the page without all of the research and angst in between. ;-)
Larissa

Proofread by Judy Zweifel at Judy's Proofreading. Cover by Literary Madness.

At Literary Madness, our goal is to create a book free of typos. If you notice anything amiss, please let us know. litmadness@yahoo.com

CONTENTS

A SNOWLIT CHRISTMAS KISS

A WARM AND WITTY WINTER REGENCY

REGENCY CHRISTMAS KISSES
BOOK ONE

LARISSA LYONS

As for the ball, so near at hand, she had too many agitations and fears to have half the enjoyment in anticipation which she ought to have had...

— JANE AUSTEN, *MANSFIELD PARK*

1

―――

SNOWFALL

———◦●◦———

DECEMBER 19, 1811...OR WAS IT YET THE 20TH?

DEEP in the woods a large wild cat sat back on its haunches and watched the snow-laden figure who'd just been dumped off his horse rearrange the two bags he'd been traveling with. A few muttered curses accompanied this effort. After more struggle than the unique cat thought the situation warranted, the grumbling man pushed to standing with only one of the valises still clutched in his grip.

The figure limped off, in the opposite direction the horse had flown, leaving the cat feeling uncharacteristically abashed.

———◦●◦———

EDWARD SNOWDEN THOMAS REDFORD, formerly of His Majesty's 13th Light Dragoons, and a third son with no intention or expectation of ever holding the title of Viscount so recently plopped on his head, trudged through the frozen, miserable night.

"Damn clouds." Covering the sky he'd expected to travel by.

"Blame horse." The one he'd rented seven miles back when the goer out of London came up lame shortly before sundown.

"Blasted misbegotten devil of a horse." The very same one that had thrown him three miles back. Startled at some strange animal cry, the beast's front hooves leaving the ground and leaving Ed—*Lord* Redford, he kept having to remind himself—now hiking on numb feet through the smattering of frost and sleet that had fallen in the last hour.

Six days of freedom. That's all that remained.

Six days before his engagement was announced and became a binding contract he could in no way break. Not without harming his family's already tarnished reputation.

A mere seven months ago, he'd been cocooned in his own wretched world of fever and pain, loss and regret, fighting for his life in Spain. And not, at the time, having a thought to spare for grieving the loss of his arm.

Four months ago, the infection waned as his body strengthened, the amputated limb suitably "healed" but his other hand crushed, and still mostly useless when he'd arrived on English shores, mad at the world—but mostly at Napoleon.

Angry with Beresford too, the fighting at Albuera bungled indeed by the commanding officer. Casualties on both sides beyond significant. "Such a goddamned waste. *Ooph!* Watch it," he told his left leg after tripping over some unseen stumbler hidden amongst leaves and snow.

'Twas coming down thicker now, the sporadic sleet turned to solid white, the cold reaching past the layers he'd donned when he was forced to leave his smaller valise behind—though some lucky soul would appreciate the two shirts, buckskins, handkerchiefs and neckcloth inside, among a few other sundry items. Not to mention the fine shoes tucked within. His ankle still did better in boots, not the dress shoes. Besides—unlike the rest of his family—footwear was easily enough replaced once he reached home.

Renewing his grip on the bag he'd kept with him, laden with important papers, a few irreplaceable possessions, money and a change of clothes, he attempted to look out, beyond the black night and glossy sheen of ice and snow covering everything, seeking some manner of landmark or hope.

Finding naught but a quick shudder through his frame as the bite of wind sunk its teeth in his weakened, sorry self. His ungloved hand too frozen to be nimble enough to work its way inside the protective leather without aid.

His booted feet moved well enough after the

months of recovery but still not smoothly. Especially not with the bitter frost seeping past the layers, numbing him from the outside in. Quite a refreshing change, that. Had the last weeks finally provided the time he needed to absorb the shocking news he'd received while continuing his recovery in London?

The letters from his mother, no nonsense, straightforward and practical—to the point of abrupt—just as his capable, efficient parent had always been. His other now? Father being something of a wastrel, an entertaining one to be sure, but a man who would rather drink port than ply himself with estate details. "Is that not why we hire hirelings? To run things for us, eh?" More interested in the Devil's brew and bouncing to London town to visit his mistress than: "Remain at *home*, eh? Not with your mother always going draconic on me, criticizing everything from my waistcoat to my wine choices."

Mayhap, if his father had not slept in his waistcoats nor sought out the most expensive—smuggled, of course—wines to be had, Mama would not have issued complaint?

No matter. Not now. Not with Father gone, as well as Ed's siblings.

Unlike Ed, his two older brothers had taken after their pater in disposition, and in recent months, first one and then the other succumbed to revelry: John perishing on the dueling field after dallying with a married trollop; Robert falling to footpads one recent night—no doubt too much opium and port to give his eldest brother a chance against the band of scourers.

That had been several months ago, during the worst of the fever. And now Ed was, regrettably, in possession of his mama's latest two letters, the first summoning him home: *Now that you have recovered —and your brothers have dispatched—*Ed thought he'd detected a smear over that line. A fallen tear or two? She might sound cold on the surface, but his knowledge of her contradicted that—*and with your father's health continuing to decline, 'tis past time the three of us accept the truths inherent in our situation and set forth our next steps.*

You, Ward, are now your father's heir and will soon hold the title. (Very soon, my dear boy, given how he continues to guzzle tipple, despite Dr. Callahan's orders to the contrary.)

Which means, along with the estates and what monies your father and brothers have not yet squandered, you have also inherited the betrothal he arranged years ago between Robert and Miss Larchmont, Lord Ballenger's eldest. She is a tad long in the tooth by now— Robert kept postponing the marriage, you see, quite unwilling to honor it though your father pressured him so —but you can make things right.

Oh, could he now?

*There is nothing wrong with her that I can tell—*if his mother thought she was reassuring him on this front, she was sadly mistaken—*and supposedly, money changed hands years ago, when the betrothal was first drawn up—you may ask your father about it (for I* *would rather ignore him of late—and him me. Would that I could. But nay. Between Dr. Callahan's visits, laudanum dosages, and answering Redford's demanding shouts, I am around him much more frequently than my sanity would prefer.*

There had been more. But the hard crux was, along with the title he never expected, it seemed he'd now gained himself a bride.

Though John—until spilling blood on the dueling field—had been counted quite attractive to the ladies, Robert started drinking to excess early and hadn't been in prime twig for quite some time.

Ed spared not a thought to the unknown Anne, of what *she* might be like. Rather he wondered what she might think of *him*. Of how he compared to his eldest brother, Robert. For a portly, overly pompous, selfish drunkard he was not. How would one compare that to a one-handed soldier who knew next to nothing about running estates and caring for anyone other than himself?

In gaining him as her betrothed, the hapless Anne just may have received the short end of the bargain.

A sphere of thick snow circled round his head and somehow snagged between his booted toes. A stumble. A totter. A lurch and he went down, knees landing painfully on the hard-packed sleet. Pride falling even lower.

Although... *If I freeze to death, then neither of us have to go through with it.*

There was that.

"You landed yourself in the suds this time, did you not?"

Anne Larchmont, whose younger sister Harriet persisted in calling *Merry* Anne the last two weeks —"*Because 'tis almost Christmastide and you're to be married, Anne. How can you not be inundated with joy?*"—shivered in the dark night, chest aching and arms so tired it was a wonder she still held the heavy shovel between them.

"Inundated with joy, my grieving soul." The bitter words slipped past frozen lips.

The lantern light, reflected off the recent and unexpected spate of snow, didn't reach nearly deep enough for the unpalatable task she'd set herself, the stillborn babe of one of the Spierton tenants wrapped in her temporary death shroud brimming clearly in Anne's mind.

The babe, awaiting a proper burial come tomorrow, still secure at the abode where the couple farmed for the miserable, distasteful father of Anne's dearest friend, Isabella—who Anne had come to visit early that morning, well before any hint of this fierce and freezing storm alluded to its wretched arrival.

That morning? Pah.

What had, in fact, been mere hours, seemed more like *weeks* to the heart- and body-weary Anne... Given all she'd endured since naively setting off prior to any hint of impending snowfall...

. . .

Acknowledging the unusually warm weather this close to the end of the year, coupled with her eager anticipation of visiting her closest friend, was it any wonder Anne departed her boisterous home at first light, with a decided lift to her steps, despite the nearly eight-mile walk?

Any wonder she'd applied herself the night before, convincing her mother that she was more than capable of doing so alone? Had argued that a female so firmly on the shelf—not to mention *supposedly* betrothed—should be able to amble a path she'd trod hundreds of times before. In truth, she wanted the quiet. Didn't want to spend the two-hour journey talking with her maid, no matter that she liked the girl.

With the formal announcement that decreed the end of life as she knew it looming mere days away, Anne looked forward to being alone with her thoughts. Looked forward more to visiting with Isabella, her dearest friend since childhood.

After the leisurely, if long, walk Isabella's delighted smile greeted and welcomed.

"How you chose a fortunate time to visit." Issybee's cheeks flushed with joy. "Father unexpectedly left for London yesterday, so we have the whole house to ourselves, at least for a few hours more, if not longer." Which was absolutely wonderful, because Anne had come in the hopes of spending the night.

With the cook gone to market, Isabella and Anne savored the warm embrace of the kitchen, baked goods abounding—without the Lord of the Manor to spoil the hours of stolen joy, his absence allowing the remaining household to take a collective breath now that his tyranny had eased, if only for a short while. Especially since the Spireton housekeeper, the rudesby Anne considered only a shade less unpleasant than her employer, had departed for Wales for the holidays. Leaving Anne and Isabella free to laugh and confide and talk of any manner of important or trivial things.

"Tell me, do," Isabella encouraged after the two had gathered a smattering of biscuits, breads and cakes and settled themselves inside of the open door to enjoy both treats and a coze. Or in Issy's case, to enjoy the slice of sunshine beaming in from the outside, Anne helping to tug one chair *just so*, so that the bright ray fell upon Isabella's ankles.

"Let me know what you are wearing," Isabella encouraged. "And then describe mine." She stuck out one foot and lifted her skirt several inches, showing pretty pastel stockings. Anne thought the left one ecru while the other appeared pink. "I never know what I have pulled from my wardrobe these days, what with Papa being so stingy on servants, and letting Alice go."

"He didn't," Anne gasped. "Did not even let you retain your lady's maid?"

"I do not mind, truly," Isabella said, and from the look on her face, Anne could do naught but believe her. "Her presence was pleasant enough, but it had to have been a huge bore, serving me, as all she ever did was help me dress and undress. No matter that I would have taken solace from country walks or perhaps just feeling the sun upon my face, Father insisted those were unnecessary frivolities and made her assist Mrs. Wynn during the middle hours, which we both know could not have been agreeable." Of course it wasn't; as youth, they had both called the termagant that presided over Spierton when its foul lord was away *The Warden*. "Though in some ways I can see Father's view on this. It wasn't as though I am oft leaving the grounds and need accompanied."

Isabella Spier...Issybee, of the dark ringlets (when she had a lady's maid, that was) and the pale green peepers—that didn't see a speck. Whose rotten awful arse of a father refused her liberty to visit anywhere since her sight dwindled to naught, practically kept her chained inside Spierton no matter that, like Anne, Isabella was deep into her twenties and well able to care for herself—as long as she was familiar with her surroundings, or had an understanding companion to guide her. Anne ached for her dear friend, locked in not only the prison of her blindness, but in the prison of her wretched father's making.

Still, impending engagement or not, she had to do something to help her friend. *What if your future spouse confines you every bit as much—*

Nay, that didn't bear thinking of. Neither did Issy's situation.

"Only because he won't let you," Anne said, all the venom in her heart bleeding through her tone. "It should not be said aloud, but I hate your father. Hate him."

"Mind your tongue, dear." Isabella's voice, by contrast, was soothing, as was the touch of her fingers upon Anne's clenched fist—after a short search over the table between them. "Some days, we know not who else may be listening in."

So her friend was being spied upon now? And in her own home? "'Tis unconscionable!" Anne railed, never so frustrated with their lot in life. Alas, for someone with excellent eyesight and more freedom than many females her age and station enjoyed, some days it seemed to Anne as though her choices were almost as limited as her blind friend's. "You should return with me posthaste. I am sure *my* father would—"

"Nay. My place is here."

"Dash it, Issybee, your place is—" Anne swallowed her frustration before she choked on it. "Forgive me, dearest. 'Tis almost Christmas. Let us chatter over lighter things."

She would bring the subject of Issy defying her father up another time.

Anne foraged in her reticule. "Here, I brought you a little something." She placed two long ribbons within Isabella's fingers. "Satin. Griffith's latest arrival." She mentioned the emporium the two of them used to visit together in years past, before her friend became naught but her father's prisoner. "One is a brilliant red. The other a deep blue."

Isabella laughed. "Excellent. Now we can play." After enthusiastically finishing off the last of her biscuits, she held up the blue ribbon and ran her thumb and fingers over it for several seconds. "This one is red."

"Right you are! Here. Again." Anne took them both in her hand, trying to stifle laughter, and placed the blue one once again in Isabella's fingers. "And this one?"

"Red again. You thought you could play me false? Hand me the blue one."

Anne gave over the red ribbon, smiling widely and so very saddened anew that her friend couldn't see and share in the mirth. "Can you tell any difference?"

"Not one whit. I have every confidence you have just spouted clankers through your teeth."

"Me?" Anne's voice conveyed pure innocence. "How could you even think such—"

"Mrs. Wells! Welly! I need help!" A small tornado burst through the door they'd left open, stumbling to an uncertain halt when his young face beheld not the cook he'd expected, but instead the Lady Isabella and her guest.

"Owen?" Isabella surmised. "Is that you?"

"Yessm." The child sniffed, his brown eyes swimming in tears and redder than the ribbon Anne had just placed on the table. "It's *Mama*," he cried. "But she's been trying for hours."

Isabella held out her hand and the boy who looked no older than five came right up to her and climbed on her lap, an occurrence Anne had no doubt would have brought forth harsh and criticizing words had Isabella's father witnessed.

"Your papa?" Isabella asked in a soothing tone. "Is he at home, helping—"

"Gone. With Lord Spier. To Lunnon. What do we do?" the child asked on a loud snuffle. "Doc Fielding is away."

Only it came out sounding like, "*Docfiedway!*" as the child's sobs intensified.

"How may I help your mother?" Anne asked with every confidence, positive that something could be done to assist this tragically crying child who ripped holes in her heart and made her want to offer up her lap as well.

"She's breeding," Isabella shared in an aside, "and from what I hear, bigger than one of Prinny's carriages."

Snickering at the image her blind friend painted, 'twas a moment before Owen's claim sunk in. Any humor at the situation vanished. "Your father took her husband, knowing her time was near?"

Blind but beautiful green eyes rolled toward the ceiling as Isabella gave a light shrug, frowning, and rocked the crying child.

"Lord Sp' told Papa they'd be back t-today. And

sweet L-l-lord..." Owen now sobbed in earnest. "Lord G-grayson...he died."

"Oh dear." That news seemed to worry Isabella more than the rest. "It sounds as though your mother could use some support."

"Lord Grayson?" Anne asked. "Is he recently moved in?" And now... Deceased? So soon? Before she'd even met him? Her heart wept for the unknown gentleman, young Owen's grief palatable between them.

Isabella gave a slight shake of her head and beckoned Anne closer. In a hushed voice, patting the back of the child, she offered clarification.

"Ah," Anne said when her friend finished. "That explains much." Dusting off her fingers, flicking a stray crumb off one of her half gloves, she stood. "Is there a sister, cousin, anyone else we can call on?"

"N-no one!" The child cried harder, his small chest heaving.

"I will go. Be with your mother until your father returns." Though she could list his faults as many, Lord Spier tended to be punctual; if he claimed he would return Owen's father today, Anne was confident he would.

"Are you certain?" Isabella placed her hand on Anne's arm, gripping once she found it. "For Owen is correct; Doc Fielding is on holiday with his family. Let me ask a servant to go in your stead." Isabella wilted, her arms tightening around the sobbing child. "Who, though..."

Who, indeed. For Anne knew Spiderton (as she

preferred to think of the difficult man who had sired her dearest friend) tended to employ either very young or very old servants, paying them only a pittance.

And had she not assisted with several births herself? Granted, most had been of the four-pawed variety, but still. With young Owen here, odds were the mother-to-be knew just what to do and only needed a spot of assistance. "Nay," Anne assured, giving Isabella's shoulder a squeeze, encouraging her friend to stay seated. "I have attended the birth of countless animals and two humans." Did her older cousin having twins count as two? "So consider myself more than up for the task."

"You'll come help?" Sniffles and wet eyes couldn't detract from the youngster's relief.

"Of course I will."

Not to mention how Anne herself expected to be married soon. Something she kept trying not to think about. Except the idea of her own family, her own children—sprites as outrageously outspoken as her sister Harriet—beckoned. Had they not, she'd have rescinded her agreement long before now. As it was, Anne had given her promise to at least meet the new viscount before jilting him.

Pah. She'd been betrothed to his older brother as long as she could remember, and the only good thing she could say about Robert was that every time he wrote to postpone the marriage (not any more inclined than she, or so Anne surmised), she had to bid herself not to write back and *thank* him.

"It will be grand practice for my own brood," she told Issybee, gathering her reticule, cloak and outer gloves. Wishing she'd brought a warmer bonnet, she tied her straw one beneath her chin. "I am planning seven, you know."

Isabella smiled, the old gash above one eye glaring in the light streaming in from the open door. "Seven? To match Harriet's latest batch of kittens?"

"Exactly. I shall assist your tenant till her husband returns and then make my way home."

Isabella helped the young Owen off her lap and to his feet and stood to hug Anne. "You are the very best of friends. Visit again soon? You know you are always welcome."

When Lord Spider-wretch was gone. "Of course."

WHAT HAD SEEMED A SIMPLE, sensible plan twelve hours ago had proved itself the height of folly. Owen's father away longer than expected. The birthing infinitely more difficult.

The lantern near Anne's feet flickered. The hole it shadowed barely deep enough to bury a thimble. Night had fallen hours ago and still she toiled, determined to complete her task before the lantern's comforting glow gave out.

Anne's lungs burned from the cold—but more from the shoveling. Fingers and toes long gone numb, heart not anywhere near—that frustrating organ persisting in heaving with grief and sadness—

not to mention the blasted shovel—with every labored breath.

Humming one of the carols Harriet was forever singing at the top of her lungs, Anne renewed her sore hold on the heavy shovel and brought it down.

"Umph!" Another hard clunk against resistant earth.

2

SNOW SHOVEL

⎯⎯⎯⎯⎯●○●⎯⎯⎯⎯⎯

Upon realizing the figure had only one working arm, *one* hand to grip the bags he traveled with, guilt assailed Phineas. Made his rare indulgence—that of a good roar to startle the odd traveler—not very satisfying indeed.

No help for it now.

It wasn't as though *he* was in a position to chase down the man's runaway horse and return the beast. Not when he was cursed to be one himself.

Nay, he'd do best to retrieve the remaining valise, see what treasures the man might have left to add to his collection. Failing that, he'd do better to watch over the errant traveler, at least see the man came to no further harm before reaching his destination on this cold, loneliest of nights.

THE INDUSTRIOUS WOMAN caught sight of Ed's approach and yelped.

Screamed, more like, the high pitch ringing in his ears even as she jumped back. The shovel she'd wielded thumping to the ground.

"I mean you no harm," he said with swift assurance, wishing now he'd taken time to tidy his appearance before setting off this morn. He likely looked a vagrant, hadn't bothered with a shave in weeks, not since an attractive nurse had taken a blade to his cheeks but failed to get a rise out of his sword. "Your lantern"—he gestured toward the inviting glow beaming from its perch near her feet despite the growing flakes that attempted to subdue it even now—"it proved a beacon on this dreadful night. I—" Ed broke off as he gained a better look at her. "Good God—you're bleeding."

She startled and looked down, a frown marring those tremulous, shadowed lips. "Nay. None is mine."

No longer lightly humming, her voice was flat, now that he'd scared the scream from her and she'd taken his measure—to the point of not fearing him. Were he in her shoes, a lone female, the shovel would be gripped tight and aimed for his head.

"Whose, then?" he wanted to know. For filth and red so dark it looked nearly black ruined what once might have been a fetching dress.

The lantern's light danced and dimmed,

spreading its weakening glow over her stalwart form. In weather like this, she should have been freezing, huddled within the confines of a large cloak, hatted and mittened. Instead, no cloak nor gloves were to be seen. Her filmy dress sleeves had been rolled up, revealing surprisingly slender arms given her current task. Why was she digging—at this hour?

"Your cloak?" he inquired. "Gloves? Where—"

Dismissing him as one might a chirpy cricket, she retrieved her fallen shovel and heaved the pointy side straight drown into the earth.

The contact jarred up her arms and shook her entire frame. "I delivered babes this morn—"

"You bloody well did *what*?" Now he was the one yelling. Near to screaming. He wanted to wrench the shovel from her grasp, bid her lay down—to rest. To grieve, the fist clamped tight around his heart telling him the reason for her onerous task.

She gave a humorless laugh. "Forgive me. I misspoke. Based on your reaction, you assume I gave birth. Nothing of the sort. I assisted one of the tenants." Despite the dark, the breezing flakes that plowed between them, that hit fabric, stuck, then melted, he could see enough.

Bedraggled strands of hair neither blonde nor brown sagged around her face and over one shoulder. Cheeks flushed, perhaps more from exertion than the cold. Jaw tightly held. Eyes—an indiscriminate color—hard. Shiny. Grieving? Exhaustion?

She glanced down at her ravaged dress and

gestured along its soiled front. "It was a difficult day."

"And night too, it seems." He gripped his traveling valise tighter, taking comfort from the solid thump of it against his calf, her travails mitigating those that had mired his brain the last twenty miles or more. "I hesitate to ask, given the state of your dress, but Mother and child?" Children, perhaps? "How do they fare?"

His simple question brought it all back—the hours of hope and excitement followed by those of fear and worry. "Who—who are you?"

Why had he come upon her—now? In this remote part of Lord Spier's estate, bordering that of Lord Warrick's on one side and Lord Bedford's on the other?

Anne visited frequently enough she knew most of the tenants, by sight at least, and Isabella had made no mention of anyone new to the area.

"A strange noise scared the beast I was riding," he answered, "and I fear my borrowed steed made off the opposite direction."

"You lost your horse?" She had not the energy to chuckle at his misfortune. Her aching fingers clutched round the shovel's narrow shaft. The wood may have long been worn smooth by hands much stronger than hers, but holding tight as it slid through her fingers, time and again, now her blisters had blistered. Anne picked at a swollen, tender one near ready to rupture and offered what little solace remained in her weary bones. "And on a night like tonight? 'Tis a pity you are not much of a horseman."

"Indeed. Not anymore." His self-directed frustration was apparent in the grit that accompanied the words. "For I would have long since found my bed for the night. Pardon. Damn. Pardon again. Should not have said thus."

What? *Bed?* Another tired chuckle threatened. It was refreshing, to have a man be unguarded with his utterances.

Though his outer clothes appeared of decent quality, they had certainly seen some wear. She was half tempted to ask him to remove his coat, let her crawl up in it and sleep for a week.

His traveling bag was too nice for a rover. But what meant more to her than his outward trappings, was that she didn't sense any manner of ill intent from his direction. Each time he started to step close, he backed away, as though aware they were one man and one woman, alone, and he didn't want to intimidate her.

More than that, his speech, though blunt, a bit crude for a man to speak so in front of a female, was uttered with fine elocution. This was a man who had seen some spot of formal education, either through a tutor or mayhap he'd been sent off to school, attended university.

All of that together, as well as the reprieve from her disheartening task made Anne, perhaps, more receptive than she should have been to a stark stranger. But nevertheless...

"I am not a young and squeamish miss to complain over a bit of forthright speech. Please be easy on that count." A long yawn forced its way past her throat. "Now I beg *your* pardon. It seems the horridly long day has sapped whatever strength I awoke with. Pray, what is your destination? Did your rebellious horse land you far from that bed you seek?"

"I am bound for the gamekeeper's cottage on the Warrick estate."

Oh, so a new employee after all.

Her chest, sick from grieving, sore from shoveling, expanded further on a breath of relief as that knowledge only confirmed her assumptions.

"Might I hope," he continued, "I have not ventured too far afield?"

"Not too. Though you have cut across Spierton lands on your journey, I confess, 'tis a boon not to be out here alone any longer." *Alone with my troublesome thoughts.* "And to answer your earlier questions, Mother should be fine. Some time and rest, and I believe her heart and body will heal."

He stepped forward, made as though to reach for her, then the valise at his side thumped back against his leg when he paused, shifted in place.

"Her heart needs healed?" All casual ease wiped clear from his face, his somber tone now expressed every bit of aching sorrow she'd felt the last few hours. "The babe died, then?"

"One of them, yes."

"Twins?"

"Amazingly, nay. Triplets. Which is why I am here—doing this."

"Wait." He swallowed hard. Audibly, across the brief expanse that separated them. "You are not —not..."

He came up and with one booted foot nudged the shovel's blunt-tipped blade that had stilled between them.

"Trying to bury the stillborn child?" she hazarded. "No. The father arrived home a good hour ago—or was it three? I'm not certain of the time anymore." She fingered the ribbon near her waist, where it dangled, now empty of the timepiece that typically resided there. "In addition to covering for an absent father and assisting a laboring mother, I cared for their scared five-year-old and caterwauling toddler."

The ticking novelty shared with the siblings, a distraction, a comfort, one she hadn't the heart to retrieve and take with her when she left.

Snow drifted between them, heavier now than it had been before. The light dance of flakes across her uplifted face both a balm and yet another worry—how would she make it home in this?

Thinking of time... "Time to get on with it."

She gripped tight and heaved, but as though it possessed its own will, the shovel wrenched itself from her clasp and descended into the earth with a thud. Anne sagged against the handle, the only thing keeping her on her feet.

"If I may be so bold"—the stranger's hearty voice washed over her—"what in heaven's name has you out in this weather—at night—digging, then?"

For all his coarse bluster, he had a soothing presence about him, a quiet demeanor that drew her. In the slanted light given off by the lantern at her feet, she saw a strong jaw covered in bristle. The face of a traveling man, more than a bit beat and one that hadn't seen the side of a blade in days, if not weeks.

It was difficult to ascertain, given the shadows of the night, but his hair looked to be a medium brown, darker than hers but not black. Of his eyes, she could confirm nothing. Nothing beyond the thick horizontal slash of his brows.

And since when do you notice so much about a man?

Since always, for not many crossed her path. *Isn't that the truth?* Other than the males she'd grown up knowing or chanced across in the nearby village, hers had been a mostly solitary existence, her father eschewing trips to London, save for important parliamentary sessions and votes that he incurred alone, her mother happy to stay in the country and avoid the smelly, soot- and sewer-filled city.

"No response, hmm?" He shifted, came one stride closer and paused. "Really, madam. You are beyond exhausted and would be better served—"

A loud, wild cry sounded close and they both jumped.

"Damn. Pardon. What the devil was that?" He

spun outward, evaluating the shadows beyond the meager circle of light. "And now that time appears paramount—before you fall down or we become a midnight feast for unsavory predators—why the devil have you not sought your bed before now?"

As though to emphasize his dismay, the lantern cracked, buzzed, flickered and went out.

"A PROMISE." The two words sighed from her in a feeble fashion and—by the sound of it, by the blazes —she lifted the blame shovel once again.

Did he press for more?

Nay, for all he saw was the memory of her done-in image. Utter exhaustion in every ramfeezled line yet still her bearing compelling. Her very self inviting. Intriguing.

Someone to take his mind away from the commitments and responsibilities that so unexpectedly weighed on him now.

Someone who—as odd as it might seem, given the current state of what all ailed him—needed his help. At least tonight.

Without thinking it through, he dropped his bag and stepped forward. "Here. Allow me."

Fumbling in the dark for the shovel he'd last seen her propping herself up with, he said, "Permit me to introduce myself. Captain Edward S—"

Nuh-uh-uh. Lord *Redford, lest you forget.*

Still unused to the notion that *he* now held the title, that both father and older brother had recently perished...his middle brother not much before that, Ed stumbled over the introduction, his searching fingers falling back to his side. Shoved into the pocket of his coat.

Was it any wonder he delayed his inevitable arrival home?

Thrilling at the unexpected reprieve when one of his recovering fellow soldiers and friends offered the use of his hunting lodge and/or gamekeeper's cottage for however long Ed wanted to make use of them? "Might need to banish a fair bit of cobwebs and rat nests," Warrick had advised, smiling grimly through the pain—his own body suffering from the same battle that felled Ed. "But I won't be in a position to enjoy either for some time. Places are both sitting empty now that my gamekeeper decided to brave Canadian shores and ended his ten-year reign at my country property. It's yours with my blessing."

And given how Warrick's estate was a mere half day's ride from Redford Manor, the offer seemed too serendipitous to decline.

Once his horse proved fickle, Ed had decided in favor of the cottage over the lodge. A full mile closer according to the map and directions Warrick had shared, along with the warning, "Just one piece of advice? Stay clear of Spierton lands. Man's an arse in buffoon's clothing. Your stay will prove more relaxing if you avoid his vile reach."

Easy enough. Avoiding people he could do.

A few more peaceful days to himself before he descended on his ancestral home—for the first time ever as Lord and owner—and Christmas descended upon him, all pointy holly and sugary wassail, suited him just fine.

But now? To find himself possibly coming to the aid of one of Lord Spier's tenants? Mayhap he could consider *this* his good deed for the holiday season, use it to mitigate the guilt he felt for making his mother wait a few days more for his arrival.

"Captain Edwards"—her voice reached through the past and brought him firmly back to the present —"though one might wish neither of us out on a bitterly cold errand this night"—she was woefully out of breath, yet still continued to struggle with her task—"I confess to being relieved by the presence of your company."

Captain Edwards? Ed decided right then he would remain thus for the rest of the night. He'd become Lord Redford soon enough. "And you?" he queried. "Your name should you be inclined to share it?"

A woman, one alone, might not be.

No chaperone, no maid, so despite the quality of her speech and manner, she must be as her laborious task and stained attire indicated: a somewhat educated tenant or servant for the unmet, unpleasant Lord Spier.

"Mary...so claims...younger..." The increasing wind ripped away the rest of her words.

He raised his voice. "Would that we could have met under more serene circumstances, but nevertheless I remain most pleased to meet you, Mary.

Relieved to meet anyone on such a cold and stormy night."

"Ann," she corrected. Ah, so he'd missed part of her name. Easily enough remedied. "Maryann..." the stubborn woman confirmed. She talked louder as the storm around them refused to ease. "To hear my sister..." The syllables muttered to a halt as her shoveling labors increased.

"Nay. Pause now." Withdrawing his partially thawed hand from the warmth of his pocket, he aimed for her shoulder, found it in the near dark and lightly traversed down her arm, taking possession of the shovel as snow swirled between them.

Finally, did she pause, relinquish the heavy tool into his care.

What now?

What now, indeed.

Using his body to maneuver it toward the shadowed hole where she toiled, he prayed his healed fingers would hold firm, not let him embarrass himself further. Grappling with the handle and shaft, he did his best to lift it for momentum, then let gravity carry it downward, still startled by the pained curse that left his lips at the effort.

Of course, that would be when the gusting wind decided to subdue its recent charge, letting his weakness ring loud between them.

Hoping to distract her from his puny abilities, he queried, "So, Miss Maryann, is there a *mister* expecting you home tonight?"

· · ·

Ha. A mister. One waiting for her?

The notion made her laugh. First one absent "suitor", and now a second? Ward doing all he could to avoid showing his face and form before the holiday. When her agreement to wait expired.

"Not any longer." Not ever, for when he did finally appear, she had full intention of ordering him right out of her home and right back to London, no matter that the more time she spent with Lady Redford and at Redford Manor, the more she could picture herself living there.

"The only one expecting anything of me tonight is Owen." Her cold hands finally free, she knuckled frozen tears from her lashes, the five-year-old's sadness still near the surface. Sheer determination the only thing keeping her upright at the moment, despite the perceptible lift to her spirits now that she was no longer alone. "And Lord Grayson, of course."

"Lord Grayson?" 'Twas a grunt, the stranger's exertion with the shovel as noisy as her own had been.

"Owen's cat."

"Who—" She heard him plunk the shovel in the ground and straighten. "Is Owen?"

"The Timmonses' five-year-old."

She really should have prepared herself. Shouldn't have been surprised at the seconds of silence, interspersed by a fresh wall of sleet and then another curse. Followed by another, coarse swear. And then—

"*Lord* Grayson? We're doing all this *for a cat*? One

that's not even yours? In the middle of the blessed night? In a lull between snowstorms?" The more he uttered, the more insane her actions seemed. "Damn fool woman—you have been pounding the frozen earth for a blasted feline?"

She refused to acknowledge his vocal ire.

"A blame *cat*?" He refused to stop. "Of all the asinine, totty-headed, inconceivable, incomprehensible—"

"Incomprehensible?" Anne exploded. "How dare you malign my task, not knowing all the circumstances that surround it. Why, how some gamekeeper—"

"Returning soldier."

"—returning soldier *turned gamekeeper* thinks he has the right to criticize the well-intentioned efforts of a stranger—"

"Well-intentioned? Madam, do you not mean ill-conceived?"

Ill-conceived? Anne sputtered, cursed the night, the timing and Lord Spier all over again.

But she could not deny how the longer they argued, the more her exhaustion melted away as she hotly defended her questionable actions.

Had she ever spoken with such candor before? With anyone beyond her family or Isabella?

Not that she could remember. Certainly not with a *man*.

How very freeing. *How exciting.*

"I may be here in the dark digging"—for what

feels an eternity—"but at least I did not fall off my horse! And then lose him!"

"Did you even ride today?"

"Nay! I walked!"

WALKED! Walked!... Walked... Walk...

Her strident claim echoed between them, the sound horribly loud against the background of silent snow and stinging sleet.

"My," Anne ventured softly, "that was loud."

"We both were."

"I do not usually...express myself thus."

"What? By arguing with people you know not?"

"By yelling."

"How does it feel?"

"To yell?" She never yelled. She'd never thought how it might feel. To do so now seemed peculiar in the extreme.

"To yell," he clarified. "To argue. To live, release the strain of today. Any of it. *All* of it." For someone who had contributed to her frustration, who had hollered just as loudly as she, he sounded remarkably composed. "How do you feel now?"

"*Marvelous.*" And she did, this unexpected spot of freedom, with the cat-hating grumbler more liberating, spontaneous and downright satisfying than anything Anne could recall being in years.

"Want to do it again?" His voice came from just over her shoulder and caused an odd thrill to shoot through her belly.

"Do what?"

"Yell at me."

"Nay." She smiled. "'Twould be horribly improper." But it was delightful to be asked such a thing. She grabbed for the shovel that had stilled between them, only to encounter his fingers instead.

He twined one around two of hers. "But I rather covet the thought of making you feel *marvelous* again. That is what you said, did you not?"

"You know I did." Her hand heated, twitched against his. *How very brazen of me.*

Perhaps this is what frees you more than not? The strange circumstances.

Nay.'Twas the stranger himself.

"Then rage!" he encouraged, hollering, "Rage at me! Howl at the night!"

"I fear I am not the howling sort," she said in an admirably calm voice that belied how her insides howled at his nearness. How her eyes, having accustomed to the dark, watched his outline, his manner with avid intent.

"Shall I do it for you?" His perfectly level tone nearly made Anne think he requested her to partner him in a quadrille.

"Do what?"

"This. *Aaaaa-oooooooooo! OOOOOOOooooooooooo—*"

And the imbecile howled at the missing moon, howled like a jolterheaded idiot, loud and long, tickled her serious side until she started to giggle. She, Anne Athena Larchmont, long in the tooth, short on charms; a lonely, nearly-but-not-quite engaged spinster; covered in dried blood and child-bearing muck; sad, tearful Owen on her conscience;

dead, skinny cat not far from her frozen feet, began laughing so hard she couldn't stop.

Not until she choked.

Coughed.

Made herself lightheaded from lack of air. And still she laughed.

Until she cried.

Then quieted.

Slipped her tingling fingers free.

Swallowed. Became her typical somber self, doing what needed to be done.

Spying it beside his feet, she bent and tugged the heavy, hated shovel back into position. "Thank you for that. Your wickedly inappropriate mirth. 'Twas a lovely respite from a horrid day. My chest aches anew but, for once, not with sorrow. I have not laughed that hard in an age. Now, really, you must be gone. I have a hole to finish and precious little energy remaining to see it to completion."

"Come now, Maryann," he all but barked at her, any modicum of amusement hardened into derision. "Do you not see the folly of continuing tonight? I thought you possessed more nobby wits. Show some sense, woman."

That odd noise rumbled and roared from the dark, louder than before. She leaped toward him—even as she began her own chastisement—aimed securely his direction.

"How dare you malign my efforts! That poor, sweet boy... His entire family has suffered enough today! Evil Lord Spier demanding Mr. Timmons join him on an overnight excursion with his wife's time so near. Her, having to suffer birthing assistance from a near stranger—and novice. Losing a child today. Having two newborn babes to care for—another to bury? And sweet Owen who braved the unknown, seeking help for his mama when she went into labor this morning—while trying to dig this very blasted hole? For the cat she raised from a kitten! All because her son's beloved Lord Grayson died during the night? You have no right to criticize me, Mr. Edwards, no right at all!"

3

SNOW KISS

<hr>

THE FEMALE'S MUTTERING CONTINUED, along with a few choice phrases Phineas surmised 'twas best he couldn't hear clearly: "imbecilic clodpate...selfish... arrogant male species... Cats have souls too..."

Her ire, though in no way directed toward him, still managed to rouse the shame that seemed determined to besiege him this evening. Rarely did he venture this far from his home woods on the far side of Lord Bedford's estate, finding the London-bound lord away from home sufficiently to give Phineas free roam over most of the extensive grounds.

Alas, *why* had he chosen today, this close to Christmas—the tenth that he'd spent on his own and away from any of his family, any of his kind—to venture further afield?

Ahhh, yes. Boredom. *Loneliness.*

The very emotion he sensed tickling the awareness of the two figures wasting their futile struggles on the frozen ground. If he could just prompt them gone, he could make quick work of the excavation, attempt to assuage his guilt over the irritating horse.

The horse. Hell, by now, he half wished he'd just eaten the blame thing. Saved himself another hunting trip in a day or four.

⸺◦⸺

VEXING WENCH, she was still determined to wield the shovel? *Tonight?*

Despite his irritation with her, how she made him laugh. Had he ever howled for a female before? Ever howled—at all? He chuckled even now.

By blazes, it'd felt good, watching her cackle, get so tickled at his tomfoolery she laughed herself sick. He couldn't remember the last time he'd laughed like that—

Oh yes, he could. With Warrick, while recovering in that ward and bandying about their broken bayonets.

But with a *woman*? To relax to such a degree that mirth blossomed so swiftly? Nay, never.

Interesting, how behaving the fool proved a boon to his downtrodden spirits as well. Having precious little interaction with females not of the doxy class— camp followers and the like—he found conversing with Maryann astonishingly easy.

Would the refined, composed (boring, he

supposed) Larchmont chit his mother lauded put him at such ease?

Doubtful. Would they even find anything to speak of? Any manner of common ground? He, with his years of war, his keen interest—despite today's bungle—in horses; she, with her long betrothal to his brother, and not much else—to speak of, naught that he knew about.

Make this *one your mistress.*

Tempting. But nay. He was his mother's son more than his father's, and he could not, in good conscience, fathom setting up a mistress before even meeting his intended.

Why not?

Why not indeed?

Not anymore, she'd responded when he inquired after her man, if he waited at home for her.

Though she was young for a widow, judging by her voice and the inky glimpses he'd had thus far, it did explain much—her independence, her determination to take care of herself and others.

"So no children?" he asked, glancing skyward, the thought of her alone more disconcerting than it should have been. Were the clouds thinning? The air turning colder?

And blast him for even asking. For even having the thought.

"Other than the two healthy ones delivered today? I have assisted with several others—if one counts the furred, four-pawed variety, but alas, none of my own."

Which was a shame. "A competent, interesting lass such as yourself? Do you not want a brood of your own?"

"After today, Mr. Edwards? The hours of crying and pain I witnessed, the mess and the sadness? I do believe I may simply claim my sister, Harriet, as my one accomplishment and not try for any of my own."

He wanted to argue with her—but that was absurd. He knew next to nothing about her—other than that he wanted to know more. Wanted to know the press of her capable, alluring body against his broken own.

He wanted to taste her lips and a whole lot more...

He shook himself from that flight of fancy.

"Your sister?" Compassion made his voice hitch. "Have you been tasked with rearing her? Suffered parental losses of your own, then?"

"Nothing of the sort. Forgive me for indicating such. 'Tis only that Harri is beyond a handful. Takes Mama and myself to keep her from scandalizing all who cross her path."

Ah, so his widow had returned to the bosom of her family. "At least you are not alone."

"Hardly ever. If one disregards moonlit digging." Neither of them commented on the missing moon.

"And babe delivering," he added.

"Ha. If you think I was alone during that wretched ordeal, you, sir, need to revisit your mathematics lessons."

The ease with which they spoke amazed him.

Ideal mistress... Some evil, distracting part of his mind taunted.

Nay, he refused to entertain the notion. For she did not seem the sort to sit around, waiting for a man to call upon her one or two hours a week.

Two hours a week? By the blazes, if she were yours, you'd see her substantially more than that.

He would.

But he couldn't.

Not and give his estates, his family name the attention they were due. Not and give his marriage and Miss Larchmont a fair chance of not being pure misery.

Lusting after another was not the way to begin their association.

But that is how it will begin, eh?

As though the remembered burn of her tantalizing touch—her fingers within his—flamed to cinders his resolve, when he heard the shovel's blade strike sodden, stubborn earth yet again, he wrested it from her. "Give me that."

What a cork-brain! Offering to bloody help on such an asinine task—and in the middle of the night?

In the snow—and resulting mud. And all for a blame mouser?

And him—with one blighted hand?

And there it was, in all its ugly glory.

The core of what ailed him these last weeks: ineptitude. Regret.

Embarrassment.

"I vow," he grunted, turning his body at an awkward angle, hoping in vain for a sturdier grip on the shovel. "If I'd known what an imbecilic task I was setting myself to"—the aborted stump of his arm slipped against the metal and he swore, viciously—"I never would have sought out the beckoning lure of your lantern."

"Stop that." She wrenched the handle from its loose position against his middle as he cursed the tender stump and white spots whirled in front of his dark vision.

Fire burned up his arm and into his neck and he prayed he wouldn't lose consciousness. Faint face-first—and sore body—in the pitiful hole they had managed to spoon out.

Then he realized that the shovel was gone and she was there—cradling his broken arm—metaphorically broken, that was—within her palms, brushing her sure, soft touch over his person—in such a way he wondered if she might soothe his broken spirit as well.

"'Tis a recent loss, is it not?" She kept on *touching* him, for God's sake. The gentle probe from her fingers reaching through the dark and chill and fear —that he'd never be the same, never feel like himself (or like a full, complete man) ever again—

He damn certain felt now. A host of inappropriate things.

"*Now* you're going to be exasperatingly silent?" Though she sounded rather vexed by that notion, the dangerously soothing caress only stroked up his arm, to his shoulder and neck, feathered over his jaw, his lips... His bottom lip. His top. She traced them both. And by blazes if his blade didn't stir anew.

His good—er, remaining—hand shot out to shackle her wrist. "Just what are you doing?"

The harsh, chastising growl that should have emerged sounded more like a whimper.

Damn his needy soul.

WHAT ARE YOU DOING?

Anne ignored the strident protest.

"Your lips are cold." The inane statement whispered between them and even with his fingers upon her wrist, she kept touching...

Exploring...

What was she doing? "Wondering how you might kiss."

The supple, chilled lips beneath her fingers trembled. Firmed. Then parted to chide, "Maryann, you cannot say such a thing."

Her stomach swooped and circled.

Did its own little illicit waltz as she caught a whiff of the man. The strength, despite his recent injuries.

Beneath the cold, the weariness of the day, the sadness and joy, the fear—delivering three babes while comforting panicked child, wailing toddler and distraught mother had roused such a cacophony of emotions...

Anne wasn't used to feeling so very raw—ever.

Anne, the responsible, dutiful, *afraid to dream, or hope for more than pleasing her parents* daughter, for once, allowed herself to be a little reckless. "I cannot say such a thing? No matter that it is the truth? Then mayhap I shall only *do* such a thing."

All right, a lot reckless.

Needing to banish the sorrowful memories of the day, the anxious thoughts of the future, she stood on her toes and replaced her questing fingers with her lips.

And you claim yourself a dutiful daughter?

Could one's conscience hiss in outrage?

Aye, Anne! It fully can! Would you abandon your virtue on a whim?

Nay, not fully, but she would surrender to a kiss. For had not sensible Anne agreed to *everything* asked of her in recent years?

Her father's words of years back rose to taunt and tease...

"Forgive me, dear heart, but this letter reminds me—from an old friend, it is. We betrothed you and his eldest upon your birth. You do not mind, do you? Never have you expressed an interest in an expensive London season." Only because her dearest friend started going blind as the two of them reached their early teens and the thought of experiencing all that without dear Issybee made the adventure fall flatter than one of Cook's flap-apples.

"Oh, Annie, dear!"—Father again, two years later —waving another letter. "Seems your Robert isn't overly inclined to marry quite yet. You don't mind putting back the vows, do you, love? The longer we wait, the more time before your full dowry comes due." A slightly embarrassed chuckle accompanied the last and she readily agreed.

Mayhap it had been to her detriment, but nay, in truth she had not minded. For to her way of thinking, Robert lacked enticements to a woman of eighteen.

But then two years turned to four and then four into eight until—a year ago, at twenty-four, why, she was more than ready to marry and start her own nursery. Be lady of her own home, despite whatever hesitations she had about the groom.

She might rub along just fine with her parents, but the older she became, the more her own thoughts and ideas—and hopes and aspirations— had to be stifled.

Because, after all, she was their daughter, dependent upon them until she became dependent upon a mate.

What a merry thrill indeed, Harriet might rhapsodize, waxing on about Anne's upcoming phantom nuptials. Her younger sister always one to exaggerate and exclaim.

But then they'd received word of Robert's demise.

And after a suitable, if mild, period of sadness and grief, rather than feeling elated that now she could find her own beau...

Or even devastated—that her long-time

betrothed (whom she'd never harbored any affinity toward) was no more, Anne only felt... Well...

Rather *apart* from the whole thing. Neither sad nor relieved, only frustrated with herself for not taking a more active role in her own future before now.

And then—only scant weeks later—Robert's father died as well, and the future dowager Redford, current Lady Redford, presented herself upon their doorstep, seeking an audience not with Anne's father—the good friend of her recently deceased spouse—but with Anne herself. "I would like above all else to speak frankly and plainly with you, Miss Larchmont, if I may?"

Startled from her Latin lesson with Harriet—whose governess had taken to bed with a cold and "yet elucidation must carry on" (from twelve-year-old Harriet herself, no less)—Anne had quickly directed her unexpected visitor to Mama's morning room. Conversely located to catch the afternoon sun, the small parlor was Anne's favorite.

Once tea had been served and the appropriate niceties observed—a second cup offered and declined—Anne placed her cup and saucer upon the table and turned to Lady Redford.

The woman, somewhere near sixty, remained remarkably attractive. Though her hair was more grey than not, it possessed a lustrous sheen, the thick mass wound at her nape, her face less lined than Anne's own—younger—mother's; Lady Redford's figure trimmer too.

"Lady Redford," Anne began, "you mentioned a frank discourse upon your arrival but as of yet"—Anne indicated their empty cups—"we have touched upon naught but the nonsensical. Please. You have traveled sufficiently to be here." By carriage, their properties were a good four hours apart. "Speak plainly, if you would."

"One moment." If anything, Lady Redford looked relieved as she reached for her reticule. After forging but a moment, she withdrew a folded letter and handed it over to Anne.

Who recognized her own writing. "My condolence letter?" Nerves fluttered in her belly. Though why should they begin now? "I do not understand."

"Your *second* condolence letter to be precise." Lady Redford exhaled audibly and relaxed back against the settee for the first time since sitting. "The one you sent when my husband passed—though you no longer had any official connection to our family, not since..."

"Since your son Robert"—*my erstwhile betrothed*—"passed on. Aye. But why should this particular letter bring you here?"

"Without allowing myself to speak ill of those no longer with us"—which had all sorts of questions clamoring in Anne's mind—"let me say that your letters, in some small way, conveyed to me who you are—as a person. A lady. Leads one to speculate, rather accurately I do believe, what manner of daughter-in-law, *what manner of viscountess* you shall make and..."

The older woman's eyes took on a distant cast.

Just then, Beatrice, Anne's one indulgence—a grey and white tabby—hopped up next to her mistress. "You baffle me, ma'am. As you say, with your son gone, there is no longer any connection between our families."

Bea gave a *merrowww*, then jumped over to their guest.

"Aye, but there should be."

Just as Anne started to cringe at her normally reticent pet's forward behavior, Beatrice climbed into the lap of the distracted Lady Redford and started kneading.

The regal woman's eyes focused once again, spearing Anne intently with their gleam. Lady Redford removed her glove and stroked her fingers against Bea's sleek fur. "My third and youngest son has now inherited everything and completely without expectation. It is my fondest wish he might inherit you as well, or at least the betrothal, as it were, to you."

"That is absurd." Eyes widening, Anne slapped a hand over her lips. Then up to her forehead before lowering it and guiltily meeting Lady Redford's expression, which was surprisingly indulgent. "Forgive *my* plain speaking. But the new Lord Redford will no doubt desire to choose his own wife when the time is right. Nay—"

When Lady Redford started to interrupt, Anne held out her hand. "We both know Robert did not relish a betrothal—much less a marriage—to me, else I would have seen his face more than a handful of times in the last eight years." Anne could not recall ever meeting the youngest son, didn't remember Robert ever so much as mentioning his brother's name. "I am quite done waiting for *any* man, especially one who has no knowledge of me."

And Lady Redford now sought a permanent union between them? Absurd, indeed.

"Brava, Anne." Lady Redford tipped her head in a regal gesture. "You now illustrate exactly why I want *you* as family and for my Ward."

Ward. Certainly a more uncommon name than that of his two brothers, John and Robert. But not an enticement to marriage.

After giving Beatrice her due, in the form of an enthusiastic chin rub, Lady Redford deposited the cat off her lap and stood, walking to the window that overlooked the manicured lawn and into the brilliant afternoon sun. "What I share next will only be spoken of once. I ask that you pay close attention and heed my words as the truth they are. I also ask that you refrain from ever uttering them to another."

More startled than curious, Anne nevertheless stood as well. "You have my word."

Lady Redford spun to face her. Outlined by the window, her face was in shadow but her voice remained strong and clear. "My husband and two oldest boys were not at all who—what—I would wish upon another. John was feckless." Anne recalled an attractive, spry gentleman (quite the opposite of the lumbering Robert) with a propensity to flirt with outrageous abandon. "Not cruel, but someone who sought laughter and pleasure above all else. Robert and my spouse? Selfish bastards in the extreme."

Anne bit her lips to stifle a gasp. Plain speaking, indeed.

"They cared naught for our lands and legacy, only for themselves. To be sure, Anne dear, you are vastly better off, not having married Robert. Now, Ward? He took after me—to my delight and his father's derision. Too serious by half. *Boring, insipid, without a dram of appeal.* Those and a host of other unjust, undeserved complaints were heaped upon his head once he professed a greater interest in fine literature than French brandy, expressed more enthusiasm for training horses than in chasing women. Was it any wonder he took to soldiering?"

After all that, Lady Redford came forward and wilted into the nearest chair. Away from the bright sun, Anne could see her clearly. Speaking so bluntly had been a trial; for the woman looked older than she had thus far. "I would like that second cup of tea now, if you please."

After Anne delivered the requested nourishment and a single sip had been savored, Lady Redford straightened her back and caught Anne's gaze. "Now, along with our steward and solicitor, I have done what I could. Ward is on his way back to English soil after a rather nasty skirmish in Spain that resulted in significant losses on both sides."

To Anne, it appeared as though Lady Redford

steeled herself to impart the rest. "From what I gather, Ward himself was injured, but with time will heal. I shall meet with him upon his return, tell him of you and seek his agreement as well. His agreement to *meet* with you. That is all I ask. That you each consider yourselves betrothed to the other until you meet and decide for yourselves if you shall suit. In the meanwhile, I would like to extend an invitation for you to visit Redford Manor. Let me show you all there is to love about the place and let you see firsthand its allure.

"What say you, dear Anne? Would you grant me a measure of hope—that you may in fact become my daughter? The one I never had?"

And what woman of nearly twenty-five, feeling neglected and undervalued and unappreciated would not consider an offer such as that wholly flattering? Compelling, even?

Her heart went out to the injured, unknown son Lady Redford cherished so. But still... "When do you expect Ward—erm, Lord Redford home?"

"Of that I am not certain. Could I have your word through Christmas?"

"Christmas? That's months away yet."

With a quiet dignity that nearly shamed Anne for her impatience, Lady Redford returned, "Aye. And my son has been off, fighting a war for a number of years. I do not know how much time he may require, accustoming himself to the title, the loss of life as he has known it, and the idea of a wife.

Surely, a few months or so is not an excessive request."

More than a little curious about this paragon, this youngest son Lady Redford spoke of, Anne replied from the heart. "It is not. Forgive me. I will gladly give your son until Christmas to claim my hand—if that is what he truly desires, for I can wholeheartedly confess to liking you as well, Lady Redford, and wishing not to end our relationship before it ever has a chance to begin."

YET HERE IT NOW WAS—MERE *days* before Christmas, days before the extravagant winter ball both Lady Redford and Anne's mother insisted on to commemorate the return of the lord and the engagement of their children—the absolute height of folly, to Anne's way of thinking.

Did they think to convince her she had no choice? That bringing together friends and family meant her fate was decided evermore? Never mind that December travel oft proved treacherous—were not the two of them proof of that tonight?—both Lady Redford and Anne's mother had rejoiced in the idea of a Winter House Party celebrating the season, the homecoming of the new heir and the coming nuptials intended to join their families.

How Anne's agreement to meet the new lord had become an engagement ball, she still wasn't sure. Mayhap being tired of waiting for her life to *start* prompted her acquiescence? Along with that of the persistently recalcitrant fellow as well.

Regardless, she'd expected him to show his absent face ere now. Several times over, in fact, secretly pleased with herself for telling Mama she'd be back in two days' time, was going to visit Issybee —and without her maid for once, knowing any manner of freedom would likely be curtailed by the haughty new lord. The one too vastly superior and selfish to even meet her?

Bah. If her parents thought to coerce her into accepting the absent knave, sight unseen, manner unbecoming, they were in for a rude awakening.

The wretched lord couldn't be bothered to show his face? To so much as extend one iota of effort to express his desire to consider a betrothal with her? She'd had enough of waiting. Was beyond frustrated with the miasma her life had become, not able to move forward, mired... *Anticipating* just as she had been for years.

Well, no more!

She had just experienced the most trying, saddest, *exhausting* day of her life and if she could seize a few selfish moments for herself—for once— by all that's holy, then that's what she would do!

So she arched up on her tired toes, pressed her lips more firmly against Mr. Edwards' and took no small measure of delight in the secure grip he had around her arm, the powerful, warm presence he proved in front of her, the unexpectedly inhale-worthy masculine scent of spices and musk and the outdoors brimming off his strong body.

Oh, Robert had kissed her once or twice (all right, thrice—but who was counting?). Yet only when others were around—such as the time Harriet nudged them under the mistletoe. Or when his father said with bravado and a complete lack of tact, once the betrothal came to light, "Go on, man, noodle her good! Show the wench what a man expects on his pending wedding night!"

Wet mouth. Hard lips. Poking tongue.

That's what she had to look forward to, she'd learned to her dismay, quite content to wait forever for the wedding.

And dreading the dreadful night that must surely follow if that was the sort of kiss Robert bestowed.

But *this* kiss?

No forceful, slopping tongue. No hard lips hammering against her own, cutting the delicate flesh against teeth and bringing forth blood...

Nay. *This* kiss...pure Christmas magic. The gentle, reciprocal press and retreat of his lips, the tiny supping motions he made with his mouth against hers...

The keen yearning that traveled from where he touched her mouth and wrist to flitter about her throat and belly...

The aching, beautiful, curious wonder of it all...

4

SNOW DESIRE

THE MAN who wasn't a man at all but more of a monstrous creature... The man with only a ragged memory of his past, lacking the ability to speak... The man who, despite his solitary existence, could still understand, reason and regret. He, nevertheless, possessed keen senses. Was that not what had kept him alive—if one could term this limbo sort of existence "alive"?

His keen hearing heard the gasp of attraction—uttered by the female upon touching this newcomer. Keen smell scented the unmistakable mating fragrance the couple exuded once they turned their attention from the grisly task she'd begun and came within two feet of each other.

Keener loneliness from the pair; loneliness he recognized because it matched his own.

Yet a compassionate heart lurked beneath his

beastly exterior. Kind even, if one could discount the myriad mammals he'd been forced to dispatch in order to survive, the four-pawed and hooved variety, not the upright, two-legged furless sort.

More than anything this wretched evening, after sensing the unmistakable aloneness they each emanated apart?

Well, it appeared even a lost, restless beast could find a purpose once every few months.

⸻◦⸻

You're betrothed! Ed's brain shouted into the abyss created by her stunning action. *Shall you prove an imbecile in truth and dally with this winsome lass while being committed to another?*

A gasp. A groan.

The gasp against his lips. The groan from within his chest.

Followed quickly by a prayer—that she not stop her curious exploration quite yet...

Light as a snowfall, warm as the missing sun, eager lips pecked lightly over his, traveling from one side of his mouth to the other.

A soft moan—hers.

And then she dropped back to her heels.

"There now," she said in the dark space between them. "Now I know."

"Know what?" His lips still tingled, awakened for the first time in months. Likely longer. Lower parts pulsed and throbbed. Completely out of proportion to the innocent mating of her mouth against his.

"Why, how you kiss." Said as though only a chowder-headed simpleton would not have followed her reasoning.

His fingers burned. He still held her wrist? Secured her flattened palm against his riotous heart? Chowderhead, indeed.

The handle of the shovel she gripped ground into his thigh.

"Nay, you do not," some forthright, part of him felt compelled to correct her misapprehension. "You do not know how I kiss at all."

What about the other misapprehensions? She thinks you a gamekeeper. A single man free of commitments.

And for the remainder of the night, till sunrise, that's exactly who he'd be.

He wanted to get them somewhere else. Inside. Out of the cold. Beyond the night. He wanted her horizontal—on a bed. Or perhaps, even vertical— against a wall. He wasn't feeling overly particular, so vastly relieved at the return of *wanting*, of desire, after months of apathy. He wanted to soak his sore leg, bask in a hot bath and sleep for a week.

But a bath would delay things. And a flat surface would ruin her completely—he had not that much restraint after so long without.

But a kiss? A real one?

Just might provide the succor he needed to follow through with his unasked-for, unwanted commitments. Might give him the memories and fortitude—not to mention the confidence—to meet the unknown Miss Larchmont without doubting himself—and cursing her...

Might give him the ability to face his wedding night without seeds of disquietude sewing into choking vines about his questionable sexual efficiency. Did his body command the ability to do his duty and beget an heir?

Perhaps he would stop doubting if he possessed the experience, and therefore the vivid memory, of kissing the stubborn, shovel-wielding saucebox bold enough to ask—in a roundabout way—for a kiss.

"I do not *what*?" she whispered. "Have the right to seek such a thing? Forgive me, sir—" She tilted her head down. "It has been the most trying day."

"Mary?"

"I am not—" Her breath sighed between them. "Yes?"

"Toss the shovel to your side, toward the hole—and away from the blame cat."

"Domineering gamekeeper, are you not?" The *thunk* met his ears the same moment she tried to twist from his grasp.

"Nay." His hold tightened, tugged her palm lower and anchored it at his side, at his waist. "Hold on."

Cursing his inability to cup her face with both hands, he filled his palm with her cheek, threaded his fingers along her jaw and hairline, and traced the outline of her lips with his thumb. Giving no quarter —for he sensed she wanted none—he angled her head up to his and claimed her mouth.

Opened his over hers, his tongue swiping a horizontal swath across the seam of her lips. Then again.

He released her mouth. Stared at the blackness between them that should be her face. Took a breath, and returned for more.

Lips covering hers, tongue sweeping—and there!

Aye. Satisfaction rumbled through him when her lips opened. At the next swipe of his tongue—still outside her mouth—she moved closer on a tiny moan. Her fingers fisted in his shirt—when had they delved beneath his coat? Her other hand wound behind his neck, gripped the ends of his hair as her tongue met his. Echoed his actions—touching his, then lightly dancing over his lips.

His heart thundered far faster than the simple kiss warranted.

Selfishly, for this was all she'd asked for, he wanted to feel her breast, cup its fullness in his palm, test its weight against his fingers, circle her nipple—after pebbling it—with his thumb. But when he moved to do so—

When he lifted his arm to caress her there—it waved in the air. Floundered. Touched nothing. Certainly not the warmth of her body.

For his was gone.

His damn hand no more.

And his other seemingly glued to her cheek. To her softness. Her heat. Her exasperating, alluring stubbornness.

Frustration made him careless. "Give me your tongue, damn it."

"What?" He sensed more than saw her pull back, lick lips made sensitive by his own. "What do you mean?"

"I no longer want a teasing, slow kiss," he said with a reckless abandon foreign to him since before he'd gone off to fight Napoleon's dangerous tyranny.

A pressured edge hardened his tone—and his resolve. "Either give me your tongue and a real kiss or be gone."

What are you doing, Ed? Trying to frighten off the first female to look at you since you left Spain piled in a cart?

"A real kiss?" His plan—if it were to intimidate her away—wasn't working worth a farthing. She returned, closer than before, her hand upon his nape weaving higher through his short hair. Her other, winding its way from his chest around his side to his back. Standing on tiptoes, practically climbing up his chest, she squirmed, then stilled. A beat of silence deepened the moment between them. "Show me, then."

Her words tumbled him back into passion's snowy abyss.

He didn't forget he was likely kissing a sedate widow. Didn't forget every moment in her company only tempted him to further liberties. Didn't forget —with his planned engagement—he had no right to take things any farther with this particular female.

He just didn't care.

"Where are you bound for the night?" he asked instead of giving into temptation, more afraid than not if he started, he wouldn't stop, not until he had her spread in the snow.

His duty as a gentleman, he should abandon such thoughts and escort her home, but devil take it, the day and half the night had worn them both to dust. At the moment, he wanted nothing more than to collapse into bed and sleep till he grew cobwebs. "Do you live close by?"

She hesitated and the rest fell from his lips, unbidden and unplanned. "If your abode is not within easy reach—and mind, the snow is picking back up as I speak—will you join me at Warrick's gamekeeper's cottage? Tomorrow morning, after rest and food—hopefully a thaw, dare we hope—I shall dispatch your vow to young Owen and bury yon Grayson."

She hesitated again. So... "My promise to you, Maryann. I will see the cat safely entombed. Come now, there are still more hours to sunrise than not. Would you share them with me?"

Would you share them with me?

Ed's chest tightened on his held breath as he awaited her reply.

Just what do you think you are asking?

Anything. A few hours, another kiss or three.

When just a few short months ago, he'd despaired of ever walking again without assistance, much less *wanting* again...

To be here—now—on his own two feet, both

working, was nothing short of a miracle. Add in the *wanting* of the lass? And unfulfilled desire 'twas a bodily discomfort he would cherish forevermore.

How did Warrick get on this close to a holiday meant to be celebrated with family? He, whose legs suffered far more egregiously than Ed's... His comrade in arms, also severely wounded at Albuera last May? His friend who'd given him the use of his property, one small justifiable delay before Ed returned home to take up every ounce of responsibility he'd never expected...

"At least if you go," Warrick had said from the sickbed next to Ed's, "I can tell my mother her efforts were not all for naught."

Mothers. He and Warrick had bonded not only over lingering injuries from the same battle, but over the bane of being burdened—er, blessed—with unusually caring maternal parents. Ones who refused to accept anything less than full recoveries for their sons.

Well, in Ed's case, as full as one could be—with one-fourth of their limbs lopped off. Add in the crushed hand, multiple broken bones in the one that still remained, the injury to his hip, two breaks in one leg... And it seemed he had a great deal to be thankful for these days.

In Warrick's case? Poor chap still didn't know if he would ever walk again.

"Trade you my right hand for one of your legs? Even the one you busted to pieces?" Warrick had proposed after the painful journey home, once they'd reached English shores and found themselves occupying the same regimental hospital—that is until their pair of draconic mothers had swooped in to move them both to a private, rented home with a personally hired physician and care all round the clock.

But before their joint maternal transfer and orders to "recover or else", he and Warrick had suffered along with the other injured in the large common room, taking solace in each other's presence.

"A leg," Ed had rejoined, the area surrounding the retrieved and removed projectile that had gouged and become embedded in his hip still fresh enough to cause significant pain. "Either one?"

"Aye," Warrick groaned, his strong arms pulling his upper body over until he reclined on his side, facing Ed. "A working one, if you will. At the moment, I have neither." The canister shot lodged near his friend's spine deadening the feeling in both even now, weeks later.

"Hell, man, you might as well have bartered for my twanger."

Warrick grunted. "Hmmm. Half my arm for your prick? Is it working?"

"Pisses just fine."

"Not what I mean." Warrick's downturned expression and the flagging hope in his eyes evident as he tracked the bustling movements of the prettiest female either of them had seen since Spain—the young wife of a fellow officer—scurrying around the man's corner bed to see to his comfort and that of others nearby.

They'd both commented on the comely woman, especially after a recent visit and boisterous chasing after her two-year-old had emphasized her attractively plump aspects in all their jiggling glory one afternoon.

Seeing where Warrick's gaze landed once again upon her "aspects"— and admitting his own body's decided *lack* of response to the lovely visitor, understanding dawned. "Oh-ho! You want a poker up to prigging? Afraid I cannot help you there, my friend. Since the battle, mine's good for making water and naught else."

Warrick swore. Then again. "Damn French frogs."

Damn *war*, to Ed's way of thinking. "Least our eyes can venture appreciation."

"Aye," Warrick agreed somberly. "Unlike Leonard's." He referred to one of the many soldiers lining the cots in the large room. Poor Leonard, with his eyes covered, wicked scarring visible both above and below the bandage wrapped firmly around his forehead.

Shifting again to his back, biting back a groan at the effort, Warrick slid his gaze to Ed's. "But I do admit, a peppy pestle wouldn't be amiss."

"A jolly John Thomas."

"A happy hammer."

"A fortified frigger."

In the end, that sick sort of laughter struck them

both. The kind that releases tension and feels remarkably satisfying even when one felt rotten about laughing over what had caused the amusement to run amok.

In the end, Warrick had swallowed wrong, nearly turned blue trying to catch his breath through gasps and guffaws—made a hundred times worse when the frisk-worthy female in question bustled to his aid, brandishing water and back pats along with coos of comfort. A palm to his flushed cheek, a hand to his heaving chest, a kind word or three as the coughing attack finally stalled to silence.

In the end, Ed watched, a bit wistfully, as his friend enjoyed the feminine attention—even if for all the wrong reasons. And when she nodded at Warrick's thanks and took herself off, back to her husband and their hushed corner, Ed speared Warrick with a glance, aiming his gaze at the area of the man's sheet-covered, groin anatomy.

"Anything?" his voice rasped, reluctant, desperate hope stifled for both their sakes.

Warrick frowned. "A flailing fish on the line would be more primed to poke."

"Ah. Damn." Was there hope for either of them?

"Aye. I cannot decide what is worse—never bedding a fine wench again, or the title ending with me."

Ed thought back to the lively, determined-their-sons-would-recover conversation between their respective mothers when the two women had visited last, how they cozed over the generations to come—

once their "boys" healed. "Or the lifelong disappointed glances for not providing grandchildren."

"There is that."

After a full minute of silence, Ed caught Warrick's gaze. "Hang our mothers' disappointment."

Warrick nodded. "Hang the title."

As one they finished, "*Wenches.*"

Of a certainty. *That*'s what they would both miss most, should their bodies fail to cooperate with their parents' dictates of *full recovery and nothing less*: Bedding a wench. *Wanting* to bed a wench.

"I keep telling myself"—Warrick lifted the sheet and shot an irritated look beneath, then let the light covering fall back—"concentrate on walking first. The right lass will no doubt stir things back to life."

"Least until then, you can attempt to fetch mettle on your own," Ed grumbled, raising his left hand and giving the distorted fingers a jerky wave. "Never have I claimed any rhythm with my left. And since the horse landed on this arm? Sometimes feels as useless as the one that went missing."

"Which, my fine Lord Redford, brings us full circle. Again I say— Either of my hands for one of your good legs?"

"Go prig yourself," Ed said, laughing.

"I shall if you shall."

He could chuckle about it in the weeks since. For time had been good to him, returning a good portion of the dexterity back to his once-crippled left hand, even if it did ache abominably in cold weather. And his hip and leg? Recovered even better. Though the limp was noticeable, especially when he overdid—as he most definitely could be accused of doing today —it wasn't horrid. Really, not even something that bothered him overly much. He was simply thankful he'd arrived back in England with both of his lower limbs, and in working order.

And if the crooked fingers or limp bothers your new betrothed?

Then to the devil with her, for Ed knew full well the value of life and was thankful for his, as imperfect as it might very well be.

Warrick hadn't been quite so fortunate, still praying for first feeling and then strength to return to his legs. Still firmly in that Merlin's chair when Ed had left London. "Use the lodge," Warrick had pressed. "Or the cottage. Mother insisted on readying them both for the holiday, hoping I'd make the trek with a few friends. Now, I ask you, what would I do in the country? I have a difficult enough time getting around in London and my doctor is here, along with plenty of amusements close by. Go. Give yourself a few more days' peace before you descend upon your family in all their noisy, welcoming glory."

If Warrick could see you now?

Arms—nay, arm—wrapped around a willing lass? Your eager stand the happiest of hammers, primed to poke...your John Thomas jolly to be roused and ready to roger.

5

SNOW STRUGGLES

"Would you share them with me?"

Anne imagined the husk of his breath between them, the night so dark not even the vapor visible.

Share the hours until sunrise with him? This blustery yet refined former soldier returned from the continent in search of—

What?

Peace, mayhap? Healing? A spot of tenderness?

Have your wits gone begging? You cannot be considering—

"No matter that I might wish it," he interrupted her mental musings, "I do not mean anything untoward. This eve, I ask for your company. To—"

That wild thing cried out again, causing Anne to hug him tighter. "What is that?"

"I know not," he spoke with haste, "but all the more reason for you to accompany me, so I can find shelter and warm our frozen selves with a bit of nourishment."

"Food?" He'd mentioned it twice now. That thought alone was enough to compel her to cry *Yes*.

You forget yourself!

Nay, for once, she was thinking *of* herself.

"Simple fare, naught but bread and cheese," he said, "but filling nonetheless." His hand slipped from her face, exposing her cheek to the biting cold, when he squeezed her shoulder. "So... I?"

Now that their fiery embrace had eased, her body burned with cold, shivers assailed, knocking her teeth together. Knocking any sense into your noodle? Seemed not, because... "Yes. Time, tonight, I can grant you." Grant us. "And I confess, after everything that has come since I awoke today, food and secure lodgings will not come amiss. But come morning," she said with conviction, "I must return."

Time. 'Tis all he asked for after all.

And if he demands more? Once you find yourself alone?

If he demanded more?

Anne doubted that he would *demand*.

In all honesty, he wouldn't need to. If he asked for more, she would be very tempted—

You would play the harlot for this stranger?

Nay. But she might consider playing the woman for herself.

"We have both been foolish to remain outside for so long and—"

That petrifying roar sounded again, followed by a strange, rough purring noise, something she might think her cat Beatrice would make after eating a herd of mice, that came from within the trees, calling Anne back to her purpose. "Lord Grayson! The hole—"

How could she be so selfish? The lure of a warm bed—*do you not mean a warm* man?—sufficient to snaffle her wits and send her into a veritable fluster over the thought of escaping the cold and retreating inside. *Getting a chance to, perhaps, sample his kiss again?*

She dropped to the ground, flailing her hands as she sought the shovel. "Where in heavens is—"

"Stop," he commanded without moving, just as she touched the handle.

"But I found it." With a bit more clumsy than she might wish, she gained her feet.

"Mary, I will see the blame cat buried at first light. Or first thaw, to be completely accurate. I promise. Hand me the shovel." She did—for it was easier than arguing.

"Can you retrieve the animal?" he asked, taking hold of her hand after transferring the shovel to his other side, gripping it under his upper arm. "The last thing either of us need after all this is for Lord Grayson to be some wild thing's dinner."

"That isn't amusing." She gave a sniff, leading him over to a large rock, where she'd left the wrapped frail, furry body.

"It wasn't meant to be." He released her fingers

and waited while she gathered the animal close. "You have her?"

"Him."

"Oh, for God's sake."

She bit her lips at the smile that threatened. "Have you a plan?" she asked once she knew her tone would sound even, though for some inane reason she was still battling humor. "You know where we are going? How the deuce can you see?"

"Language, my dear Maryann. Language. Follow close now."

"Ha. As if *deuce* bothers you. I daresay you routinely use a host of worst oaths. I should know, Mr. Edwards, for I have heard you use any number of them." Ever since the lantern gutted, it had been the darkest night in memory.

He tripped over a root and cursed; Anne's arms huddled over Lord Grayson.

"What the bloody hell makes you think I can see?" She could tell part of that was for her benefit and released the tight hold on her laughter. "How I wish your lantern still had oil."

As it hadn't been hers, but borrowed from the Timmonses', Anne didn't see the need to comment. Reaching for his back, she grabbed on to a fold in his coat with her free hand, her other cradling the cat, stayed only a pace behind. "I am not usually out so far from home"—what an understatement—"and would have been quite undone had I remained on my own tonight. I admit, now that you have redeemed your churlish beginnings, your presence has been most welcome."

"Churlish beginnings? My..." He grunted as he turned, using the side of his shoulder to forge a path through some dense brush, holding it back so she could precede him. "My spirits soar at that most enthusiastic of compliments."

In order to squeeze through, Anne reluctantly released his coat. "You are most welcome."

As was the unfamiliar tingling that persisted in her lips, the odd pressure of her tongue upon the roof of her mouth... The backs of her teeth... The soaring, dizzying sensation still rioting through her middle, each one enhanced as she brushed by his body, taking care not to drop the nearly frozen feline.

"Hold a moment. Let me get my bearings." Once through the thickest portion of vegetation, he paused and looked up and out, waited for a low-hanging bank of clouds to drift until a smattering of distant stars revealed themselves, ascertained the moon's location by the brighter haze edging upward from the horizon, still just a sliver, shifted his direction about fifteen degrees and continued on.

While she waited, a couple of fat flakes drifted down between them, not that she could see them, but she felt them hit her kiss-warmed lips, thought a couple slid against her forehead.

"You, madam, are remarkably self-sufficient." To her surprisal, his strong fingers gathered her own as he maintained a slightly slower pace. Mayhap, for her sake...? she couldn't help but wonder. Or for his own?—his limp becoming more pronounced. "Had I not stumbled toward your light, I have no doubt you would have managed.

"As to your earlier question..." His fingers tightened upon hers, and after glancing at the cloud-studded, meagerly starlit sky again, he gave a nod and now walked on more open ground with purpose. "I do believe our destination for tonight is not overly far. Mayhap a quarter mile? Perhaps a bit farther. And look yonder"—he gestured with their joined hands—"the moon is rising. Between that and our own determination, I daresay we shall make decent time. Bear with me, Mary, I shall have you warmed up in a trice."

She really should correct him on her name.

Nay. 'Tis better this way. Steal your hours in his arms, you lusty harlot. Come morn, Anne needs must return.

JUST HOW HE would accomplish that—seeing them both safely warmed up in a trice—Ed could not help but wonder. But it seemed important he reassure her. Reassure himself. Even though niggling worries pelted him as hard as the renewed snowfall...

No servants to haul or heat water.

No fire in the hearth.

No guarantee he was going the correct direction, and had estimated the distance accurately as well.

Just an overwhelming desire to fall into bed and

sleep for a week—after swiving her to squealing satisfaction.

Pity he had—for the most part—decided to act the gentleman.

<hr />

Ed had worried for naught.

His years in the military... His years romping the Redford estate grounds as a boy... His knowledge of the moon's orbit... Mayhap his need to impress the one at his side... They all stood him in good stead.

For, before exhaustion took its toll and they jointly fell on their frosty faces, Ed delivered them both to the gamekeeper's cottage.

Frozen feet, frozen feline and hungry lips aside, the next hour passed rather smoothly. Kitty was tucked away on the cold kitchen floor, near the back door where the draft coming in through the bottom would see Grayson's body remained chilled till morn. Ed quickly and thankfully had the previously prepared fire in the grate on its way to a roaring boil, heat beginning to flame forth between the two lonely souls sharing a snowlit evening and firelit meal.

As they sat there on the sturdy chaise, amidst suddenly strained conversation, the sexual aware-ness humming between them proved palatable. Made him choke down his portion faster than he should, embarrassing himself with a strangled cough, and her seeming to find meeting his eyes a significantly greater challenge than it had been earlier this evening, outside.

For himself, he couldn't stop looking at her. So he didn't try to.

It wasn't that she was a stunner, her features a little too plain, too ordinary for that appellation. But something about the way everything came together, the way he had witnessed her determination, knew of her spunk—delivering triplets, caring for young-sters, burying a cat, of all things! (he barely avoided rolling his tired eyes at the thought)—and knew how they fit together—the way her mouth blossomed beneath his...

He was captured. As surely as if she'd strung him up in a net and hoisted it over a branch, he was caught. And the lass hadn't a clue.

Her dark blonde hair haphazardly both pulled up yet falling down—again he wondered, where had her bonnet gone? Her gloves and cloak? But he was grateful for the lack, for now he could see her features in detail: the wide, tense mouth that he longed to taste again, slightly askew below the curve of her nose; the glittering eyes somewhere between hazel and grey set beneath beautifully arched brows he longed to trace with his tongue. One of her ears stuck out a little. He wanted to brush her hair back behind it, cup her cheek, smooth the flyaway strands with his thumb, tilt her face up to his and claim her all over again.

At that thought, he choked some more. Swal-lowing hard and waving her back down when she rushed to get some of the melted snow for him to drink.

Once the last bite of bread was consumed and both declined any more cheese, he tucked that away for tomorrow, added another log on the already stout fire—the action more awkward than he would have liked, one-handedly maneuvering a heavy log meant for two—and stood, walking backward until several feet of distance separated him from the temptation that was Maryann.

Still looking utterly bedraggled from the efforts of the day, yet somehow beautiful, the orange glow along one side of her face casting the rest into intriguing, inviting shadows.

"I shall leave my coat here for you." He pointed to the back of the chair where he'd discarded it after the fire's heat began reaching out. "And remove myself to the bedroom—"

"You will do no such thing." Fire in her voice, she rose and came to stand two feet in front of him. "Without a fire, any other room is too cold for sleep. I..." She cast about, her glance taking in the area with its single chair and the chaise upon which they'd resided. "I will sleep upon the chaise—only because your feet will no doubt hang off and I know you would decline it for yourself, even should I insist you take it—and you may sleep upon your coat on the floor. Either in front of the fire—or would that be too warm? Perhaps behind the chaise?"

"Managing female," he murmured with a smile.

Her solution was ideal, but— "You would trust a stranger to sleep so close? A man?"

The fire popped.

"I would trust *you*," she said simply.

"Damn. So much for ravishing you in the night."

Blast it. Had he really just said that?

Aye. For her eyes grew wide and the flush upon her cheeks was no longer just the fire.

But she surprised him once again, this lass he wished he'd met years ago, before war and widowhood took their toll, guided their lives in the direction they must go. "How can you be certain I will not ravish you?"

"I—" *wish you would. Heartily.* But he could not say that, should not even think it. *But you will both be gone tomorrow. Or at least gone your separate ways.* By hell... Why not? "No matter how I might wish that very thing, I must maintain my status as—" *gentleman.* But he definitely could not say that—for she thought him a simple gamekeeper. "Must maintain a respectful presence."

"Ah, yes. We mustn't do anything not respectful." She sounded bitter. Or perhaps only sad?

"It isn't what I would like to give you"—not even close—"but I have another shirt in my bag should you wish to change out of your stained gown. The right sleeve has been sewn; if you don't mind taking the seam out, at least it's clean."

"Improper or not, that would be most appreciated."

A glance at the metal pot he'd collected the snow

in showed it had all melted. Ed nodded toward the offering. "There is sufficient water to wash. While you do that, I will look for blankets and bring in some more wood."

He escaped quickly, shutting the door behind him to keep in the heat—to keep himself barricaded from her ever-increasing appeal.

Even her, "Your coat, Mr. Edwards! You forgot it!" yelled sufficiently loud she should be proud could not return his feet to her presence. Not until he granted her long enough to wash, change, lie down and hopefully slumber. Deeply.

Not until allowing himself to grow more frozen than the cat... But still, the lust riding him refused to wane.

In fact, only deepened to pain when he silently rejoined her nearly an hour later—only because if he dallied any longer, he feared the fire might go out —and saw how she'd moved the furnishings, to allow them both the same amount of heat, shifting the chaise perpendicular to the fire, and splaying his open coat upon the floor alongside it.

Allowing him way too easy access to herself, should his will wane as well.

Damn her.

6

SNOW SNUGGLES

WAKEFULNESS TIPTOED IN, slowly bringing Anne alert. Darkness still surrounded her. But this time, no gentle *flicker* and *pop*, the comforting sounds of a roaring fire gone silent.

Which told her as much as the chill nipping her cheeks and nose that Mr. Edwards had finally allowed the blaze to die down—after stoking it since their arrival.

Each time she'd watched with eyes squinted nearly shut, fascinated by the play of light and shadow over his strong back, the straining muscles in his forearm, visible where he'd pulled up his shirtsleeve. Fascinated just as much by the light grunts he made, shifting the heavy logs into place, how he'd whisper *blame it* or *damn*, followed immediately by a hushed *pardon*, as though even in her sleep (feigned though it was) she might take offense.

How she wanted to stroke that broad back. Run her curious fingers over those wide shoulders. She wanted to explore his chest, the muscles of his upper arms... Even the truncated arm. How bad was the scarring? Had he healed properly? Did it pain him still?

And the circumstances surrounding the injury. War, of course... But which battle? Had she heard of it? How much had he suffered?

What of the others he fought with? Had he lost friends in the same confrontation?

Her curiosity about him seemed endless...

What did he look like without his week or more of bristles stubbling his lower face?

How long would he remain as Lord Warrick's gamekeeper before moving on?

Where was he from? This shire, perhaps? Or another, nearby one?

Would she ever see him again?

And what of it, if you do? You are to be married, lest you forget.

Nay, indeed not.

For she'd come to the realization during the interminable day that she would not tie herself to a man who couldn't be bothered to acknowledge her.

The winter ball her mother and Lady Redford insisted upon could very well be held in his honor, returning lord that he was, but it certainly would not be celebrating their engagement.

As thoughts of her absent not-quite intended froze her down to her soul—perhaps aided by the blustering wind that rattled the glass panes behind the chaise—Anne realized she was trembling. Shivering from the cold. Her heated fascination with Mr. Edwards no longer sufficient to warm her.

Odd, as she recalled his deep murmurs when he'd blanketed her with bedding he'd brought in earlier. Now, huddled beneath the covers, benumbing air met her face.

Orange embers lodged beneath a heavy log were all that remained, a waft of smoke drifting from its charred edges...outlining his form, she saw when she rolled toward the quiet fireplace to find him kneeling before the spent fire, his knees bent as he sat back upon his heels. "You're awake. Damn. Pardon."

"You did not wake me. If anything, the silence did." A shudder bolted through her.

"Apologies. Still not certain how I managed to mangle it—" He swore again and she pushed the pile of sheets and blankets toward her lap, ignored the frigid air that brought another shiver and propped herself up on one elbow.

In the scant light, she saw that unlike the other times he'd tended the fire in his shirtsleeves, now his shirt was *gone*—leaving his back and chest *bare*—.

Look away!

Not on my life.

His dark hair was decidedly mussed, his brow creased and face scowling.

"Tell me what happened?" she invited.

"Damn arm... Hand..." He gestured with the

stump, ran his fingers through his hair and grimaced anew. "Damn *me*. I somehow upset the stacked, dry logs outside. Had no idea." Bewilderment may have coated his tone, but a barrage of self-loathing radiated from every word. "Amazed *that* bungle didn't wake either of us."

The fading embers struggling beneath the charred log lit one side of his face, granting a glowing edge upon his profile. He shifted on his knees and turned shadowed, haunted eyes toward her. "Cannot even keep you warm through the night as I promised. All the cut wood is wet. Soaked through. Somehow, it spilt from beneath the lean-to and now is drenched, soaked through with snow and ice and, blast it to hell and back, no matter how I try, I cannot get it to light. God *damn* it!" With his fist, he thumped his bare chest, smacked the biceps above the severed arm. "Useless."

His head drooped forward and he stared at the pile of ash and smoldering wood. "Already have we burned through the kindling. Tried using the hot coals, but the new logs refuse to take—blast me. A thousand pardons. I failed you."

"Nothing of the sort, you buffle-headed simpleton." She shoved the blankets aside and sprung from the chaise. "How long will you berate yourself for naught?"

Crouching, she wrapped her arms around his shoulders. "Stop all that useless drivel, Mr. Edwards, for you have *not* failed me, nor yourself. And you are most certainly *not* useless. Never think such. And, oh my *blazes*, but your skin is sweltering!" A light sheen of perspiration slicked the skin beneath her touch. "What happened to your shirt?"

Her hands flattened upon the heated flesh and swept outward, then came back and clutched.

You are touching a nearly naked man! Leave off. Call for the swooning-water!

Not about to faint and miss a second of this glorious experience, she found her palms eagerly stroking across his muscles... His skin... The firm, powerful presence beneath her fingertips enticing her to do so much more.

"My shirt? 'Tis snowing again. Between that and exertion, it quickly became soaked through."

You cannot keep on...fondling this man!

Oh, aye. She could.

Brazen hussy! You'll regret—

Nay, she wouldn't; Anne was certain of it. Never more certain of anything in her life. For the precious few magical hours spent with her recovering soldier and coarse-mouthed gamekeeper continue to be the most thrilling of her life.

"Idiotic man, why did you not gather your cloak?" It remained, spread, on the floor beside them. "Have you not the sense God gave a goose? For would it not have shed the moisture?" She couldn't quit touching him. Every inch of slick, hot skin proved a new discovery that sent flashes of heat sizzling through her stomach.

"Did not want to wake you," he muttered, as though remaining still beneath her ministrations pained him. "Have left my cloak here every time but realize now—"

"Have you a fever? Did walking so far in the storm sicken—"

"NAY." Ed spun toward her, tried to grab both her exploring—damning—hands with his and failed to achieve his goal. Ended up securing only one prize —one hand he clasped to the center of his chest, over his thumping heart. But he was unable to secure her other—and she kept *petting* him, blast it. Running fingers in caresses and soft, soothing strokes everywhere she could reach while her lips kept berating, questioning.

"Nay what? Have you sickened, you foolish, foolish—"

"'Tis not a fever," he told her hoarsely. He cleared his throat but somehow that action only firmed her palm against the center of his chest. "From honest, *fruitless* labor, throwing off the topmost logs that had fallen, seeking dryer ones beneath... To no avail."

"Out in the cold? In the freezing temperatures? Without a shirt? My, what an idiot!"

"Mary, you—"

"Ann," she added.

"Maryann, blast it, you have got to mitigate this horrid habit of yours you have of maligning others with your mouth! Y-your mouth..." His lips sought hers, met and lightly held. Pressed for more—but she wasn't finished exploring.

Her fingers brushed across his forehead, his temple, down the side of his neck, toward the knit-together end of his arm— She couldn't touch him there. "Nay! Do not—"

She did anyway. Caressed, searched. Stroked right over—right on top of where cut bone was covered by sewn flesh... Didn't hesitate nor stop. Feathered over his pectorals, down his quivering stomach—and kept harping at him like a fishwife. "What sort of loon, after an exhausting, trying day, spends time playing with firewood when he should be *resting*? Sleeping? Are you an imbecile in truth?"

"'Twas not *playing*," he all but growled.

"My—" The front of her palm curved against his forehead. Then she flipped it over to the back. "Are you certain you have not become fevered?"

"The only thing fevering me is you, Mary."

"Ann," she gasped, her hands now clutching the bare skin of his back, bringing his chest flush against hers.

When had he released her?

When your body decided it was ready to twang, thrum and strum again, you fool! Or did you not notice?

Oh, he had noticed all right. Now gritted teeth and fist to keep from tossing her to her back and climbing over her...

To keep himself from—

"Maryann," he groaned. For now she kissed his chest, his shoulders. "Stop. Halt." Kissed down the upper muscles of his arm. "Stop now." *No, please do not stop. Ever.* "Else—"

Her lips found his. "Else, what? You promised me a real kiss earlier. I request it now. Only..."

His mouth lunged toward hers; he forced himself to pause but a breath away. "Only... *What?*"

"Despite my actions, my forward manner, I..."

"Shhh." His mouth breezed across hers. "I understand." She could not chance him putting a babe in her belly. Did not know him sufficiently to be completely intimate. "I do understand. I want to kiss you, desperately. Shall I also confess how very much I want more? But be assured, sweet Maryann, I shall not take that which is not mine." The vow ripped from him.

"You won't?"

"Mary, please, do not sound so forlorn."

He was not a rutting beast to lose control. Did she but know it, he was a *gentleman*. And would behave as one—to a point.

"Are you still cold?" Her teeth had stopped clattering.

"Nay. I am fevered as well—for you."

Ed fell back upon his cloak, tugging her with him.

"See now? My pantaloons are on. Fastened too." Damn it all. "Climb on me—*Ah*...aye." An apt pupil —or mayhap simply a hungry widow—she rested her torso over his, her legs sliding—

Sliding...

Oh God grant him strength. How could he have forgotten? She wore naught but his shirt? Her bare legs slid between his and her fingers touched his bottom lip as she breathed hotly. "Like...so?"

Oh, sweet heavens, yes. "Just like so."

He palmed the back of her head and meshed their lips.

As though the hours since their kiss by the abandoned grave a mere moment, her tongue thrust alongside his, stroked, retreated and returned.

His lips melded against hers, tongue surging with a gentle yet starved motion. For *this* was the sort of kiss he'd longed to give her. To receive.

To experience together.

Her unbound breasts plumped against his chest, calling to his mouth; the heat between her legs beckoned like a banquet to a starved man. Yet Ed, despite his need for more, contented himself with granting her kisses upon kisses. Magical ones, if her squeaks of excitement, her murmurs of *mmm* and *more* were to go by.

Forced his loins not to lunge, his pike not to plunge—thankful to be alive—and with her here, back on English soil; relieved to know he could—physically at least—twang and hammer and swive.

But not tonight. Not with his stubborn, merry widow...

So ardent kisses it would be. Loving her with his mouth and naught else.

Her fingertips scratched through his stubble, latched on to his hair, held his cheeks, his neck, his shoulders as their mouths danced and dueled. Tasted and tantalized beyond anything in memory...

How this woman could kiss!

But then the sharp points of her nails gripped hard. Fastened against skin.

Their sensuous kisses paused as she tongued the delicate skin beneath his throat.

Her restless legs shifted, no longer content within the cradle of his. She straddled him and arched—and through the barrier of his pantaloons, she started riding his erection.

And he? So stiff and hard and excited for her it didn't take but three earnest swings of her body and damn if he didn't blow, didn't melt right there beneath her, snug within his pantaloons instead of her heated, honeyed treasure.

For the second time that night, Ed saw stars.

White spots that swirled behind his eyes. Whirled in front of his head. Only this time, 'twas caused by the bounty in his arms, the one who squealed out her own release, rode his spent hanger with jerky abandon and renewed her kisses upon his lips. His cheeks. The stub of his arm…

Tears and stars spun together, and for the second time in his life, he lost consciousness.

Only this time, it wasn't under a brusque surgeon's saw but beneath the loving acceptance of a lass he couldn't have. Couldn't keep.

Of a caring, cat-cracked lass every bit as unattainable as his five missing fingers…

AFTER KEEPING watch over the outside of the cottage where they'd retreated...

After gleefully, if quietly, spilling and spreading the stacked wood beyond the lean-to intended to keep it dry (utterly brilliant idea, that)...

After ensuring the couple within would likely exhaust the supply already inside...

Mayhap—dare he hope?—huddle together for warmth...

The four-footed observer decided he had done what he could, regarded his efforts here complete and returned back the way the three of them had all traveled scant hours before, one last, remaining notion to see accomplished before he too sought shelter and slumber.

7

SNOWY SUNRISE

AWARENESS CAME to Anne in a flash.

The very emptiness surrounding her told her she was alone. Had her loonish companion traipsed outside to again battle the fallen pile of logs?

At the thought of him, a gentle smile curved lips still swollen and sensitive from their many kisses.

The early-morning light was meager, just a faint hint surrounding the window edges. She let herself drift, not yet ready to stir, to relinquish the peaceful contentment flooding her body, the sensitive, satisfying ache weighing loins.

He must have placed her back on the chaise? For she was snug amongst the covers once again.

She remembered naught after falling asleep upon his chest, accomplished only once he'd startled awake after a few frightening moments of stillness, hugged her to his heart and breathed deeply, his sigh of repletion echoing her own.

Her last thoughts focused on the gentle way he brushed his strong hand over the still-trembling contours of her linen-covered back. Trembling no longer from cold but from the dazzling array of new sensations streaking through her. His broad palm stroked down again, this time his fingertips lingering lightly where his shirt ended and the naked curve of her thighs began...

Harlot!

Anne smiled. A slightly wicked, wholly wanton, drowsy smile to be sure.

After she'd been thoroughly kissed—and *enjoyably*, for the first time ever... After she'd experienced more physical pleasure than she'd expected...

Than you had a right to. Harlot!

Recriminations might come later. For now, her limbs—and areas between—felt entirely too satiated, too replete for her to care whether she'd behaved the strumpet or not.

You did!

Then good for her.

<hr>

THE NEXT TIME SHE WOKE, the light permeating her eyelids confirmed the glorious night was no more. That their stolen time together had come to its conclusion. Blinking tired eyes, Anne rolled over on a silent sigh, disappointed to see the room empty of his presence.

With a slow stretch, stifled by the narrow chaise, she reached for her watch, dismayed to find the ribbon empty. Everything rushed back: the grief, the fear...

The sound of a hundred *drip-drip-drips* pattering from the rooftop—heralding the melting snow—interrupted the disturbing recollections. Brought forth, instead, wondrous ones from the last few hours.

With the door shut and no discernible sounds coming from beyond, she made quick work using the chamber pot, rinsing the sleep from her face—with the remaining snow melt—and reluctantly relinquished his shirt (though not before inhaling the scents lingering upon it an embarrassing number of times) in exchange for her grimy dress.

Oh heavens, Mama would have hysterics the moment she saw the state of Anne's dress. Well, there was no help for it.

Fortunately Anne had let her hair grow longer than many her age, and it was a fairly easy matter to take the stringy, snow-dampened mass and coil the long strands into a knot at her nape.

The sun bursting in through the grubby window to streak across the floor fetched the surety that she needed to hasten her departure. Lest her mother fear highwaymen or brigands had made away with her eldest daughter and sent Anne's father out with his hunting rifle.

The minute she opened the door and let herself outside, her ears—along with the rest of her—wished she'd maintained possession of her bonnet and cloak, had remembered to retrieve her gloves and reticule—hidden somewhere in last night's clearing by the snow and storm. Forgotten in her concern over her task and then her encounter with her companion.

"MARYANN!"

At the hail, she looked up to see Mr. Edwards striding toward her from a rough wooden building she hadn't noticed the night before, out behind the cottage.

"You were not going to creep away without saying goodbye, were you?"

Though that had occurred to her, it had also saddened. "That was not my intention. I, um...used the chamber pot."

He smiled. "That is what it's there for."

Never again would she take for granted her maid. Having a servant to clear away such things seemed of significant import at the moment. "Yes, but... But I wasn't sure where..." *You cannot even bring yourself to say "to empty it"?*

So easily did he shrug off her concern. "No matter." He flicked his hand toward the smaller building and beyond. "I shall see it dumped out and rinsed."

Her face heated as he reached her. Heated even

more when he lifted several fingers and brushed them across her flaming cheek. "Do my eyes deceive me, or did we finally chance across a topic that the intrepid Maryann is uncomfortable discussing?"

Oh my. His eyes were blue, the striking blue of a jay in flight, whipping its wings and propelling itself forward. Her treacherous heart beat just as fast.

For they were the sort of blue one never forgot.

But you must forget!

With the sun above the horizon, she could see him clearly for the first time. The stubble that covered his cheeks and chin grew in a bit patchy, showing a couple of sparse areas below his bottom lip and on one cheek. The ends of his hair were sun-lightened, the rest a rich brown.

In the light of day, he looked wholly disreputable, delightful, and—woe to her heart—desirous.

That's not even a word!

It most certainly is! she shouted back. Now do be quiet.

She wanted to hug him. Wanted to feel the hard press of his body against hers again.

Shameful hussy.

Anne resigned herself to the truth.

For who else in her life—save Harri, who brought them up—had she ever been bold enough, comfortable enough *with* to discuss the most indelicate of topics?

"We did, I fear. The thought of..." She now gestured to the far building he'd indicated. "Chamber pot content disposal," she whispered, as though the words themselves should be banned, "not something one discusses outside of...er, family."

He laughed. "Do you forget, oh modest one, I shared barracks and a multitude of appalling accommodations with other soldiers? Bodily functions are certainly not new to me."

She bit her lips hard, had to consciously release them—and only did so when he drew one hot finger across the tight seam. "But sharing them so intimately with another is quite new to me."

He shifted closer. "If we are going to talk of intimate things, I can think of any number preferable to chamber pots."

She grinned, even as her hands crept to his chest and climbed higher, until they jointly rested upon his shoulders. *For shame, Anne. Just what are you inviting?*

She wasn't sure. But she hoped he would.

He drew his hand off her face and nodded as if coming to a decision. "I will only speak of this once and please forgive me for any perceived, though unintended, insult or slight, for that is not how this is meant, I assure you." He closed those beautiful eyes she could stare into for hours, then lifted his lids and swore. "Would that I could make you my mistress."

She gasped. Shock burning her hands off his shoulders until she clasped them in front of her chest, the sides of her smallest fingers barely grazing his coat when he inhaled. But she didn't step away. Didn't feel insulted.

You should!

She felt... Curious. Not quite flattered, but mayhap...complimented? *He has just insulted you beyond anything you have heard before.*

Hush! Anne ordered that nagging voice. Wanting to hear what else he might say, this bold, wicked gamekeeper of hers.

Oh, so now you are going to claim him? All that snow must have dripped into your ears, blurred your brain of any sense or sanity.

Or mayhap 'twas that kiss. And the hours, and others since...

"I KNOW." Ed held her gaze, felt his lips lift in a stiff grin. Was both amazed—and relieved—she hadn't slapped him for the sentiment. "Totally inappropriate, to suggest something of the sort after such a short acquaintance. To a woman of your obvious quality. Please do not be insulted."

She regarded him in such a way he was completely baffled. What had her gasp conveyed? Was it outrage? Or, dare he hope, excitement?

It matters not, you blackguard! Would you betray your almost-betrothed, one Miss Larchmont, before you ever meet her?

Should I sacrifice my happiness forevermore? For of a sudden, it seemed of great import that he speak what was in his heart—the beginnings of exactly what, he knew not. But the thought of never seeing her again wounded as surely as a blade.

All she did was scrape her teeth over her bottom lip, release it, eyes narrowed and glittering in the bright morning sun. "Go on."

"I—I…" He stumbled, fumbled about like a soused idiot with no notion of which way to go. "I like you exceedingly. And completely out of proportion to the length of our association, but when one considers the circumstances, perhaps my regard may be counted not a measure of insanity?"

Insane or not, you must end this folly now.

"I wish, fervently so, that I was in a position to see you again, but alas—"

She placed her fingers against his mouth, stalling whatever he'd intended to say. "I think I understand. Astonishingly, no insult is felt. Only a large measure of flatteration—is that a word?" Her fingers drifted down his chest. "Doubtful, but it does work for the moment."

"As have we. Thank you for the wondrous kisses."

"I shall remember those always." His Maryann spoke swiftly and blinked faster than he'd seen her do thus far. "And I must be off. I may delay no longer."

"Right." Well then. There was that. How did he remain upright and stoic, given how the burgeoning dreams he'd dared conceive now clashed and clattered all around him? She obviously cared naught for his barbarous declarations. Needed to return to her home and life. "And we cannot forget that I have a cat to bury properly."

She gripped his hand. "And to say a prayer over? Please."

Ed grimaced. His hand? Did the missing one bother her? He thought not, but perhaps—

"I know you do not like cats."

"I never claimed that." He pushed the lowering thought away. He might have insulted her honor with the mistress mention, but he'd not insult her by thinking less of their time together, not belittle himself, by trying to ascertain why she now seemed so determined to be off. "What I do not like is the idea of burying them in the dark, in the middle of the night, when it's freezing and sleeting."

"I can acknowledge that." She released his hand, grudgingly, or so he wanted to think. "I wish you safe journeys."

He gave a slight smile, trying not to cry out at the loss of her touch, more than somewhat wistful about all that would never happen. "But I remain here. You are the one journeying forth. And without escort, which—"

"Please. Not that again." More than once during their evening meal, he had offered to escort her home. She'd avoided making any specific mention of where that was, and had declined his assistance. Heartily.

So perhaps she would be ashamed at the thought of being seen with you...

But no, she looked at him, *ogled* him, still blinking swiftly. Still not moving off, despite her words to the contrary.

"Here. If you won't let me accompany you home, at least take this." He shook off his coat, with less poise than he might have wished, and swung the protective leather around her shoulders, stilling her halfhearted protests and fastening it beneath her neck. "With the sleeve severed and sewn, we cannot hope for a better fit. But at least be warm, for me if not yourself, and allow the destruction of your dress to be hidden on your return."

"Thank you," she acknowledged with a soft smile. "You are right." She glimpsed downward and grimaced. Then met his eyes once more. "I am relieved to not be strolling the countryside in such a state of shambles. For a sometimes surly grumbler, you are remarkably considerate."

"And for an oft stubborn woman—" *You kiss beyond compare.*

I will miss you dreadfully. Which made absolutely no sense, they had just met.

But he couldn't say any of those things, and while his mind blundered about, she spoke with ease. "As to your journeys? Granted, for a former soldier and current Warrick gamekeeper, you may be here. But I perceive this may not be your ultimate destination."

What a peculiar thing to say. How would she know this was only a temporary reprieve before he reluctantly embraced the duties facing him forever onward? "What makes you think thus?"

Her gaze went unerringly to his missing appendage. She reached forth and grazed her fingers down his arm and past the bend of his elbow, leaving them where the bone and flesh stopped, the sleeve of his shirt shortened and bound to cover the ungainly sight.

"You are healing. That much is obvious. I cannot imagine the atrocities you have witnessed or perhaps participated in." Her gaze veered to the side. She swallowed and then faced him once more.

Had he hit his head back in Spain? Had he lost his brain instead of his arm and fingers? Because the next thing to reach Ed's awareness was how very tightly she wrapped both her arms around him, how she crushed her entire front—from face to feet— along his hungry body and clung. Gave him the fiercest, longest, utterly best hug in memory.

She must have stood on her toes, for her lips found their way to his neck. One quick kiss. Then another. Was that her tongue? Had she just licked him?

His head reeled, senses spun, for her ardent actions roused his previously relaxed champion to stiff and standing—all the more confounding because they were saying *goodbye*.

"Be well, Mr. Edwards." Her words were smothered against his skin. "Thank you for everything. Lord Grayson thanks you as well."

Then she was gone. Her lips. Her arms. Her warmth.

Gone as she gripped the inner edges of his coat and turned. Turned and literally ran. Fled from him as though she expected to be chased and caught.

Captured forevermore. And damned if that wasn't tempting. Because bidding her farewell was wrong. An unjust mistake he had no way to rectify.

"Mary!" he shouted. Yet still she ran.

He glanced from her retreating form to his lame leg. "And damn you too."

His eyes were drawn back to the space between the trees where she'd vanished and he just stood there. Dismayed. Defeated.

Completely disconcerted by all that had occurred in the last few seconds, by all that had passed between them in the last few hours.

For somehow, it seemed—no matter how doltishly—that he had just watched his heart flee.

Not quite an hour later, with the sun noticeably higher, the last of the cheese filling his belly and poor Lord Grayson, by now completely stiff and cold himself, securely tucked along Ed's side thanks to his one good arm, he approached the site where so much had occurred the night before. Arriving at the small clearing, he stumbled to a stop.

For the hole was dug. *Completely.* Mounds of slushy earth, muddy and half frozen, piled up in a semicircle on the opposite side.

He walked slowly forward and inspected the surrounding grounds.

The shovel remained where they had left it, propped against a tree, where Mary said Mr.

Timmons would retrieve it later. A thick coat of white dusted every exposed part.

Yet, only a very light covering of snow blanketed the emptied portion of earth.

Ed knelt, gingerly wedged his bent knees in the sludge and cautiously, carefully eased his burden past his thighs and down into the hollow, lowering the frail body where it would remain undisturbed from predators.

As he sat back on his heels, thankful for once that the cold had numbed the ache from his knee, Ed used his teeth to grasp the tip of his one glove, pulling and tugging until it slipped free and he could run his fingers over the indentations that edged the top of the cavity. The ones that looked like large... Paws?

Impossible. Lynx had been extinct on British soil for hundreds of years. Weren't they? Besides, the sheer size of this print precluded that possibility.

Then what in blazes had made these?

Shaking off the odd conundrum, he leaned forward until he could place fingers upon the blanket-wrapped cat. "Journey on, dear Lord Grayson. I know you brought your people much happiness, probably your share of mice, grasshoppers and welcome purrs as well, and shit on me if I know what else to say. Farewell, sweet cat."

With only a slight grunt, he pushed to standing, stretched out his sore leg and walked over to the shovel. Shaking off the snow, he applied himself to scooping the displaced dirt back inside, and damned if he didn't hear a single, distinct *roar* the moment the first damp clumps landed upon the deceased feline.

With the oddest chill racing along his spine, and the bright sun beaming down and warming the back of his neck, Ed finished his task, his thoughts never far from the woman who had vanished from his life as quickly as she appeared.

* * *

TUCKED within the snow-drenched copse of trees, a bit further back than he'd ventured the night before, Phin watched the man finish the job of burying the cat. So plaguey, how his senses—whether he existed with two legs or four—remained so acute. For he could smell the stench of death even now, the early stages of decay. The scent invaded his nostrils, worked its way up into his brain and taunted his memory.

Memories. Something he struggled with, ever since that fateful night—

Nay. He would not think of that. For he had treasures to inspect.

Phineas had considered returning the second valise to the weary traveler.

He could have left the worn leather bag next to the hole he'd made short work of, his powerful paws and cutting claws easily piercing through the icy earth until he deemed it deep enough.

Aye, he *could* have returned the valise, and in

some small manner, perhaps made up for scaring the man straight off his horse and onto his none-too-steady feet last night, but nay.

There were so few unexpected occurrences in his life these monotonous days, that Phineas decided he would indulge himself: keep and savor whatever treats might be inside.

8

SNOWY SURPRISE

"Harriet!" Mama chided Anne's sister in a hushed tone that nevertheless carried far beyond their two places at one end of the long table. "Stop whining over your dinner. Leave off crying and *eat*, child."

Mama had lost a wager with the twelve-year-old —else Harri wouldn't be anywhere near the adults but rather up in the nursery, helping oversee and entertain the young visitors who had traveled on this brisk winter day with their families to attend the Twelfth Night Ball their parents hosted this night— supposedly to celebrate the season.

In actuality, to celebrate—or so her parents and Harri and their esteemed guest, Lady Redford, hoped—the betrothal of Anne and Lord Redford. And really, how preposterous, to call it a *Twelfth Night Ball*, when the Christmas season—and the twelve nights, had barely begun.

How ludicrous, to expect she would affiance herself to the absent viscount.

As if she would even consider agreeing to marry a lout who couldn't be troubled to introduce himself beforehand.

The gall!

The selfish, inconsiderate... Her brow lined as she cast about, unsuccessfully, for something harsher to call him.

Inconsiderate...*imbecile!*

Butterflies did not inhabit Anne's stomach. Nay, nothing so tame. 'Twas more like marauding midges inhabited her middle, causing all sorts of annoyance and angst Anne would rather pretend bothered her naught.

If she didn't truly *like* Lady Redford—the imbecilic lout's mother, soon-to-be *Dowager* Redford...*if* she and Harri and Anne's parents all had their way—Anne wouldn't even have presented herself at tonight's holiday festivities. Though the Great Hall was seldom used by their small family of four, it had been decorated to within an inch of its life and looked downright beautiful...with its abundance of fresh greenery, festive red candles and sprigs of holly tacked up around the hearth and doorframes. Overly pointy holly, she had learned to her detriment that morning, helping Harri gather more when her sister deemed the servants' efforts "not quite adequate for a party of such notable import".

Even mistletoe, tied with bright ribbons, had been sprinkled throughout the common rooms—

something Harri had insisted on, claiming what better way for Anne to celebrate with her new betrothed.

Pah. Would it be up to Anne? At this very moment? She would have already declined.

Better to be lonely—and forever childless—than to tolerate a miserable marriage for the rest of her days.

What makes you think it would be miserable? You haven't even met—

Oh but she had. She had met the sort of man she could imagine growing old with, mayhap raising a family with… But it was not to be.

For transient gamekeepers and former soldiers thought of her as a *mistress* (which even days later, still did not fail to both mystify, flatter—and yes, sadden), not as *marriageable*. Not as *mothers* for their children, but rather as a strumpet, fit to strum but not to *love*.

And whose love is it you are hankering after? You, who claim she wants no children of her own?

"Eat your goose," Mother ordered her recalcitrant youngest in a strident voice, reminding Anne of the joys of motherhood (she thought with a large dose of sarcasm), "and quit carrying—"

"But, Mama!" Harri cried in such a way everyone present was privy to the private conversation, likely even the mice, asleep in the stable walls outside. "I *knew* Sir Galahad. I walked him and petted him and —and…" The tears started rolling down flushed cheeks yet again, making the brown-haired, hazel-eyed child on the verge of womanhood resemble nothing so much as a bawling cherub. "I looked into his glossy black eyes..."

The last was nearly howled and half the guests around the table glanced at their plates and turned a bit green, while the other half bit cheeks and tongues, trying to stifle laughter.

All except for the lone empty seat, that was. The one conspicuously between Anne and Lord Frostwood—supposedly a good friend of the missing Imbecile's. Redford's other friend, who had arrived with Lord Frostwood in a Merlin's chair, had been seated at the head of the table near Anne's father, on the opposite side of the melodrama going on about the goose. These two men, at great cost to themselves, had managed to arrive from London, yet Redford himself could not be troubled to appear in a timely manner?

The man was not just an imbecilic, idiotic chuff. He was an arse. A most awful, rude one, to be sure. And Lady Redford had vowed he was the most thoughtful of her offspring? Hardly.

Mama was still in high dudgeon, chastising Harri, completely impervious to the girl's tears and wobbling lips.

"I daresay, 'tis the last time you entertain the chit's fascination with whist," Anne's father remarked in his unruffled, droll tone, the ideal counterpart to her mother's exasperated napkin toss—directly upon her plate of uneaten braised pigeon, glazed venison and Sir Galahad the goose.

"Up! Up this instant, young lady," Mother instructed Harri, snapping her fingers for the girl's governess, hovering just out of sight. "Your antics have been indulged quite enough for one day."

"Oh, do let the child stay," said Mr. Gregory, a neighbor of middle age whose even temper—if overly bland manner, to Anne's way of thinking—overrode Harri's sniffles. He addressed the table as a whole. "Who among us has not befriended at least one thing found upon our plates during our lifetime?"

"Hear, hear," said Anne's father. "For me, it was the time I realized turtle soup was just that—made from the turtles I played with at the lake." He caught Anne's eye and winked, giving away his clanker. Her father had an aversion to lakes (and snakes)—certainly would not have *played* near one as a lad.

But his response, thanks to Mr. Gregory's beginning, took the attention off Harri's tear-stained face and mutinous expression long enough for Anne to motion her sister over.

Harriet slid from her chair and sped around the table. Knuckling one eye dry, she propped her other hand on her waist. "Did *you* eat him?"

Harri's red-rimmed gaze cut to Anne's plate—where she'd covered the empty portion by creatively spreading the remaining pigeon. Anne answered in a whisper. "Of course not, dearest. Did Mama really lose two hundred pounds to you, teaching you whist?"

That had been the story, when Anne arrived

home last week, sneaking in through the servants' entrance near the kitchen and up to her room with haste, before her mother caught sight of the stranger's coat, the stained dress beneath and the disheveled state of her elder daughter and called for the swooning-water. Or mayhap yelled loud enough to do Mr. Edwards proud.

Hiding his coat at the very bottom of her trunk. Denying to herself how she couldn't stop thinking of him every time she lifted the lid and delved beneath the other contents to touch the heavy leather, wishing it surrounded her companion from that magical night.

"Actually it was closer to three hundred!" Harriet exclaimed, bringing Anne's attention back where it belonged. Thankfully, her sister's eyes had brightened. "Papa laughed in an upwar... Upwarious?"

"Uproarious?" Anne suggested.

"Aye, that. Up*roar*ious manner when I told her I would graciously forgive her debt if I could avoid the nursery tonight."

Anne chuckled, saw Lady Redford doing the same. Even Anne's mother appeared to be fighting a smile at the absurdity of it all.

Though, if studied closely, both maternal parents cast anxious glances toward the open doorway, checked timepieces with a frequency bordering on obsession, even closed eyes and—it seemed to Anne—murmured a prayer or two.

So, both mothers fretted over the missing guest? As well they should, given what a huge to-do they had made of everything. What should have been a *small*, celebratory "welcome home" had turned into a winter party of epical proportions. As to Anne, since she'd already decided to decline the tardy, disrespectful viscount, come what may, she cared naught whether he showed his missing face and form, or whether he celebrated his Yuletide not at all.

Missing the magnificent meal the mothers had arranged. For did an absent lord deserve such indulgences? The huge goose roasted and carved to perfection and taking up a significant portion of the center of the long table, the rest of it laden with vegetables and breads, desserts waiting just out of sight... Ratafia, port, brandy and other assorted beverages ready for toasting his inconsiderate carcass.

Anne would just as soon toss a few ounces of spirits on the fire, watch the flames flicker high and think of her quiet, firelit night a few days past... Her intriguing companion...the kisses they'd shared...

The kisses shared but not nearly completed— not to her satisfaction.

Did you not promise yourself you would think of him no more?

Yearning blazed through—

"But it's dreadfully boring. I had no idea."

While their guests laughingly continued to share tales of befriended table fodder, Harriet had leaned in to speak directly in Anne's ear, startling her from the indecorous notions never far from her mind.

"Dreadfully boring?" Anne repeated, trying to gather her thoughts back into a sane semblance. "You mean here? With the adults?"

One absent adult in particular whose very presence would have comforted Anne to no end. Isabella, not permitted to attend. Because her father was an arse. Kept her shuttered away as though her blindness was a blight on *his* reputation. Had Spiderton even checked on Mrs. Timmons? Given her husband so much as a day of rest to mourn his still-born child?

"Yes!" Harriet said loudly. "I said *yes*! Why are you not attending?"

Because, like you, I surmise, I would rather be anywhere else.

Anne used her arm at Harri's waist to draw her closer. "Would you rather join the children in the nursery?"

Harri nodded, her gaze slicing to their mother. "Only I want my vowels' worth. Cannot have Mama thinking she need not pay her debts."

At that, Anne thankfully laughed outright.

Her vowels' worth? Just where did her sister pick up these things?

Waving off the governess, who stood several feet behind them waiting to assume responsibility for her charge, Anne's better humor continued. "Ah... If it's not seen as horridly neglectful of me," she said, loud enough that their guests could hear while she focused on first her father and then her mother, "I shall escort Harriet to the nursery and rejoin everyone in the ballroom?"

Her parents traded a look, and then her father gave a nod.

She had put it off yet again—delayed meeting the absent Lord Redford. For there was still the dessert course to be consumed before the rest of the guests relinquished their dining chairs in exchange for the dancing chamber.

Why, at this rate, she might not have to bother with him at all this year. *If* the scoundrel even dared show his face.

"If you wish..." Once the trio reached the entrance hall, Harriet's governess spoke to Anne, gesturing up the stairs. "I shall see to Harri from here."

"Why do you not both come with me?" Harriet proposed. "We can shuffle off to my room and play hustle cap, for you are both ever so much more entertaining than the babies in the nursery."

Knowing that both of them had lost more pennies than they wanted to count playing the tossing game with Harri, Anne and the governess shared a smile, one the governess quickly subdued.

"Unnecessary," Anne told the other adult. "I will take Harri up and stay with her for a while." *Might give my confounded nerves time to settle.* "Have you eaten?" Doubtful, for the servants were often expected to wait until those they served had been seen to. "Take thirty minutes for yourself and rejoin us when you're ready."

At their continued discourse, the youngster between them rose up and down on her toes.

"You're too kind," said Miss Primrose—a name Anne always thought almost too fitting, for the young woman was as staid and buttoned up as they came and had a propensity to blush violently rose red at everything.

"Too selfish, I confess," Anne confided. "In truth, I shall savor the distraction."

Bobbing up and down like a bouncing ball, Harriet huffed her impatience. "Adults. Too boring by half."

"When we're not entertaining you, you mean?"

The women parted on a shared laugh, Miss Primrose heading downstairs for a bit of sustenance, and Anne trailing after an exuberant Harriet who already raced her way up the staircase.

Just as Anne reached the third tread, the door-knocker sounded. Anne hurried after her sister, hoping to be out of sight before the footman admitted the latecomer.

That reluctant to meet your potential, soon-to-be betrothed? For shame.

It matters not. I am saying Nay!

Harri, it seemed, had other ideas, swinging round to descend the staircase in an instant.

"I will get it!" she trilled loudly, announcing to anyone and everyone within the house.

"Harri, no," Anne admonished in a hushed whisper, but too late.

As she stood there, only six steps up, her sister

sped past the footman and swept past their butler, who reached the landing coming from downstairs—slightly out of breath, a napkin in his hand and blotting his mouth.

At least someone had enjoyed Sir Galahad's sacrifice.

Harri swung the door wide, blocking Anne's view.

"Who are you?" Harri demanded through the open doorway, making no move to allow their visitor entrance.

"Lord Redford, at your service," a strong voice intoned.

A familiar voice that sent Anne's stomach scurrying to her toes. "Come for the Twelfth Night Ball, if I am not mistaken, though a few calendar days early by my count, but here I am, dates notwithstanding. Do you require my written invitation?"

Harriet just cocked her head. Wilson, their butler—used to the outrageous frolics of the youngest Larchmont—seemed amusedly inclined to let her handle things.

"What happened to your arm?" Harriet wanted to know, now gazing upward. "Where's the rest of it?"

"Harriet!" Anne gasped, her feet flying faster than her common sense, landing her next to her sister, staring at the tall, well-dressed, smoothly shaven gentleman, top-hatted and looking rather shocked at her appearance.

He wasn't the only one. Her coarse-speaking

gamekeeper spruced up beyond well, if her galloping heart and the battling midges were anything to judge by.

"Mary!" he exclaimed, a combination of pleasure and perplexion lighting his expression.

"Lord Redford." Wilson stepped into the breach. "'Tis beyond good to see you again, and after so long. I am sorely glad to see you returned." How was it their butler knew her betrothed?

Betrothed? I thought you determined to say Nay.

"Come in, my lord," Wilson continued. "May I have your coat and hat? Your gloves? Er, apologies. Glove?"

"Think nothing of it, Wilson. 'Tis war. We all must adapt and accommodate for change." He may have spoken to the butler, but his attention remained firmly on Anne. His eyes asking a host of questions she had herself:

What are you *doing here?*

Do you belong? Or am I dreaming?

Was the other night naught but a trick? A farce?

Were those starlit kisses truly as compelling as I remember?

Or was that last one only her?

Anne found her palm and fingers cupping her lips, lest she gasp again. Or cry out her confusion.

Do you not mean your yearning? *He is here! Claim him—before he disappears!*

"Merry?" Harriet laughed and turned to Anne. "Merry! You see, 'tis spreading!"

Nay, what was spreading—based on Redford's

abruptly ruddy complexion and Anne's lightheaded-ness—was mortification. A heaping dose of it. As if he, finally, had only then recalled his near offer to make her his mistress!

The lout. Already intending to take a lover—before even greeting his probable wife?

Inconsiderate imbecile.

She *would* refuse him. She would!

As he stepped over the threshold and struggled out of his coat—refusing Wilson's aid—Harriet's smile faltered. "Your hand," she persisted, but did at least lower her volume. "Did you lose it fighting Napoleon?"

"Harri. Hush." Anne snaked an arm around her sister's collarbone and tugged her backward, against her trembling form. "Forgive us, L-lord Redford"—how she stumbled over that—"for not welcoming you properly to our home." Then she could not help but needle. "I trust your journey was a strenuous one, else you would have arrived before dinner began? Mama held it back, waiting for you but stomachs gurgled and grumbled, threatening to turn the drawing room into a rumpus."

Despite the hold on her sister, she dipped a mocking curtsy just as her mother bustled in and the man himself spoke—to Harriet, while still managing a glance at Anne. A wholly unreadable glance. "Aye. Left it in Spain, I fear."

"Lord Redford!" her mother exclaimed, approaching. "Welcome! I see you have already met Anne. Your mother will be along—"

"Anne?" His gaze swung from Harriet to her mother to Anne's now embarrassed countenance. The winter flush left his complexion as he paled. "*Lady Anne?* Not Mary?"

"Mary?" her mother repeated blankly.

Beyond the small party gathered near the door, Anne heard cutlery clinking, chairs scraping back and a renewed murmur of voices. Like a plague of locusts descending, the Entrance Hall was about to be overrun.

Arms still anchored around her sister, Anne edged toward the latecomer, rather than risk him asking again. In an aside intended only for his ears, she explained, "M-E-R-R-Y. You misunderstood. I daresay we both did."

"Rather a lot, it appears."

Be my mistress...

Those startling, gravel-voiced, absolutely flattering and wholly insulting words ran through her mind yet again.

Swoon? Yell at him? Take a swing, perhaps? Rail at her mother? Appeal to her father? What in blazes should she do?

"Where at in Spain?" Harri wanted to know. "Did you see it afterward? Your hand? The rest of your arm? Terrifically gruesome, I suppose. How much did you bleed? Do you know? Did your claret splash out? Or only trickle?" Her sister gave a bit of a shudder.

And the look on Lady Redford's face as she

approached in time to hear that last bit? Shock? Outrage?

Harri's inappropriate Inquisition likely scandalizing that kind, majestic woman to the point she, in all probability, now lamented ever seeking an audience with Anne.

Her gaze bounced back to his. Blue fire.

Then back to his mother's.

If Lady Redford knew how Anne had behaved with her son? Climbing over his bare chest wearing naught but his shirt! Rubbing herself against—

Harlot! I told you, did I not?

It didn't bear thinking about. Her face was on fire.

She had to escape.

Before the marauding midges burst free and her tongue stung everyone within sight.

But Harriet's curiosity wasn't close to being stemmed. "Did you scream when it happened? Or cry? Or were you brave? I, for one, would have screamed and probably fainted, I am quite positive."

"Terrifically gruesome," he repeated, his attention finally dragged from Anne and toward her sister. "I am sure. As to the, er...spatter, I am not certain that is a subject fit for genteel company."

"Oh, but you can tell me! I am ever so curious about—"

From headless goose to one-armed suitor, Harriet, it appeared, had found a new fascination.

"Harriet Jane!" Mama looked livid. As well she should.

"See to your guests and dessert," Anne told her parent, jaw held tight, gaze refusing to veer again toward the lout in question. "I shall see to Harriet."

Directing her sibling with an unrelenting grip on her shoulder, Anne aimed them both for the stairs.

"Lovely to meet you, Lord Redford!" Harriet called out, fighting against the pull of Anne's tugging which insisted they ascend with undue haste. "You can tell me later—"

"*Shhhht.*" Anne wrenched her heedless sister around and gave her a shake. "Not another word—do you hear me? Not until we reach your room, you frustrating hoity-toity."

9

SNOWBOUND SOLDIERS—AND SISTERS

- One pair heeled men's dress shoes, dated style (though what he would know about current fashion wouldn't fill a snuffbox)

-1 linen neckcloth, starched but wrinkled

-1 pair buckskin breeches, worn...small hole along one seam

-2 muslin shirts, ecru, with ties at the wrists and neck

-1 shaving kit that has seen far better days, still usable

-3 plain handkerchiefs, no embroidery, no ornamentation

-1 well-worn Bible

-3 fiction books, all well read

What have we here?

Searching the depths of the valise, Phin's questing fingertips met a small wad of bunched fabric crammed in one corner.

Curious about the small bundle, stashed so far down it would be easy to overlook, he scraped at it with his nails until it came free from the tight crevice. As he withdrew it, his hand fisted around the tiny, hard object wrapped within.

Placing the fabric upon his lap, he unwrapped the handkerchief, this one embroidered and old, thinner than the others but infused with so much love and care it made his chest hurt.

Phineas growled low in his throat when he unearthed the ring nestled inside, cursed, both himself and the fates, for 'twas inconceivable he render this particular treasure unreturned.

Yet another task to add to his growing list of things to accomplish—if speech ever returned to his lips. And the ability to maintain human form lasted beyond an hour or two...

⸎

NOT PLAIN, pretty Mary at all.

Not a potential mistress after all.

Definitely Not *merry* Anne, despite her sister's claims, not given the glower, the battlefield-worthy daggers directed his way from stormy hazel eyes.

Eyes that had disappeared up the stairway—along with the rest of her—before he quite knew what to do. What to make of the astounding realization that was swiftly coming to light.

He took one step toward the staircase, ready to fight off Wilson and anyone else who might try to keep him from her but was hampered when two women of similar age—one his mother—rushed toward him.

"Son." Defying her typical restraint in public situations, she came right up to embrace him in full view.

Holding him tight she put pressure on his shoulders till he dipped his knees and she could whisper in his ear. "Ward, how could you? Arriving in such a tardy fashion?"

Hearing the anxious concern in her voice, he felt ashamed for not journeying straight through. For using Warrick's to escape all that he now must face.

She squeezed his shoulders before releasing him and leaning back, a tear dripping down her cheek that raddled him like a fiver to the gut.

"I did not mean to cause you worry." He wiped away the damning moisture with the side of his palm.

"Comes with motherhood, my dear boy." She bit her trembling lips once, blinked, and it was as though her angst vanished; once again she became the capable, affable parent he knew and loved.

Had her wrinkles been that plentiful, that deep, when he saw her last in London? Or had his delinquency aged her unnecessarily?

Unnecessarily? You would have missed meeting Mary? Anne?

Nay. To the devil with guilt and regrets, he wouldn't have missed those kisses, those few hours for anything.

But how to make things right with her? The remembered look of betrayal wounding her features a second punch to his gut.

Once more, the empty staircase drew his gaze. Could he—

"You're healing nicely, son. The swelling has gone down tremendously since I saw you last." His mother had taken his hand in both of hers, was patting and petting him as though the action calmed her. But then the relaxed look on her face pinched as she clasped her fingers round his smallest one. "Where is it? Your signet ring?"

His mouth opened but nothing came out.

"You *lost* it?" said in such a way one would have thought he'd gambled away their home.

Curling his raw fingers into a fist, despite her lingering touch, he lifted one shoulder in a shrug. "Lost it. Left it. I know not which."

Her dismay brought back his own, some days prior, when he'd first discovered it was gone.

His second evening at the cottage—the first without *her* distracting company—he'd been emptying his valise, taking stock of food (none), clothing (some), money (enough), ahead of a walk into the nearest village the following morn for supplies and sustenance.

The valise emptied, a sick feeling hollowed his gut.

His thumb circled his smallest finger. *Bare.* Then again. Still bare. Then the next— *It's not there; you refused to wear it.*

"Where is it?" He grabbed the bag, turned it topsy-turvy and shook it, the blame sides flopping together until he rammed the stump of his arm inside to hold them open.

His father's—*yours now!*—signet ring. The one his mother brought him, her impassioned words echoed in the letter she'd left with him on her first visit to London after his father died.

But other than trying it on—once, and unsuccessfully due to the still-healing bones—it'd been easier to ignore. Both the ring and all it represented.

Had he secured it on his person for the journey?

Knowing it wasn't on him, Ed still patted his pockets with frantic motions, his left arm crossing his body to reach and check every one.

"Damn. 'Tis truly gone."

Had he forgotten it? Or had he intentionally left it behind?

It was a symbol of all that had changed, of all that he had assumed: the title, the responsibility of making success from the dregs of whatever his father and brothers hadn't frittered away...so many resources belonging to their family undervalued by his sire.

Was it still at his temporary London lodgings or—

By blazes. What if it had been in the other valise?

The snow and cold, his injured left side, along with his injured pride, fingers mostly frozen by then, all hampering his rushed search when he combined the two?

Every bit of remorse he'd felt then came roaring back now, staring into her not-quite condemning but definitely questioning eyes. "Grandmother's Bible." He bit his lips before finishing. "It's mislaid as well."

He'd decided he must have missed both in the dark, after yelling at his contentious horse. "Failing on all accounts before I have even started as Lord, eh?"

His mother gripped his hand—hard—and leaned back up to whisper harshly in his ear, "Banish that sort of thinking, Ward. For it is beneath you."

To anyone looking, they had been savoring a long-awaited reunion. No one but the bothersome inner voice that needled him frequently knew how very much that sentence reminded him of the other woman so recently in his life.

Told you not to let her go. Idiot.

"Lord Redford." As if deciding he and his mother had been private long enough, the other, definitely piqued matron sought his attention as she clasped hands and threw a few daggers of her own up the staircase, after the recently departed pair before returning her attention to him. "I am mortified at my youngest. *Mortified!* That is not how the rest of us go on. If I didn't know better, I would think she wasn't mine." The woman heaved a sigh big enough to ruffle the curtains across the hall. "Preposterous girl! Behaves as though she was raised in a barn by wild Gypsies," Anne's mother uttered, proving a kinship with the entertaining, forthright Harriet after all.

"Supposed to be celebrating your engagement, old man."

The deep voice he instantly recognized jerked his head toward the man striding forth.

"Frost?" The bewildered syllable actually prompted the customary grimace into a grin from the phiz before him.

"In the flesh. But back to you. Where in blazes have you been?"

Frost. He was here? The man both he and Warrick had to thank for not letting their broken carcasses rot in a soggy corner of Spain. The man who had ridden back in, onto the muddy battlefield —after the order to retreat—to locate and dig first Ed out from under the French Dragoon's dead horse, and then Warrick unmoving, his partially paralyzed body already dumped in a pile of dead soldiers. Frost, the one comrade unwilling to let either of them truly perish in that bloodiest of encounters.

And he was *here*?

Bloody astonishing. His friend not the most social or jovial of creatures at the best of times, had a tendency to morose out even further whenever the holidays approached—something Ed wasn't supposed to have noticed, he was sure.

"Why has your laggard arse been so remiss in

presenting its dawdling self?" The brusque question was accompanied by a scowl from the most welcome, frowning countenance of his oldest friend. "I made an effort to show my ugly face on the way to celebrate with my own family..." No doubt a hummer, but one Ed chose to let pass unchallenged. "Needed to meet the unfortunate female hapless enough to land you for a spouse—only to find *you* gone? Not yet arrived? And with you leaving days before we did?"

We?

"Aye!" Warrick rolled up. *Warrick had come too?* Had troubled himself to make the journey as well?

One of his hands slapped the side of the ambulatory chair he occupied. "When I arrive anywhere *before* anyone, there are answers to be had," Warrick stated. "Do explain this rumfuzzle, if you would."

Ed's head spun faster than the wheels on his friend's chair going downhill—the invalid's chair they both prayed was temporary. "By the blazes, *both* of you? Trudged through the snow all the way from London?"

"If by *trudge* you mean rode in Frost's splendid carriage, then aye."

At the reunion of soldiers, both mothers faded into the background—but Ed saw the pleased smile on Mama's face, one that gloated and told him he had her to thank for his surprise guests.

Still, for them to journey forth, at this time of year—and in this weather? Risking life and limb (which now held greater significance to Ed given his loss of one)... "I am touched," he told his friends, giving them his full attention, knowing he would explain the rest—as best he could—to his mother later. "Beyond words."

With a thick throat and buoyant heart—for the moment, refusing himself the luxury of dwelling on the lass who had fled up the stairs—Ed pulled Frost in for a hug.

Then they both reached down for Warrick. Exchanging embraces betwixt themselves, back slaps, possibly even a moist eye or two, the men not ashamed to express relieved emotions after all they'd been through, now that all three were firmly back on English soil, if worse for wear and more solemn of spirit.

"And just *where* did you stop and dally?" Warrick wanted to know once they'd each pulled back and composed themselves as a self-possessed Englishman was wont to do when in the presence of others. "And who have you been dallying *with*?" The up-and-down dance of his black eyebrows emphasized his salacious meaning. Warrick's gaze lowered from Ed's face and focused straight ahead, which for Warrick meant Ed's crotch. "Dare I hope? For my sake as well? Parts in working order yet?"

Given the presence of flourishing company just a few feet away—had everyone in the nearby shires been invited and hazarded traveling in winter?—no matter that his friends spoke quietly, uncomfortable heat flared through Ed's face. "Not yet. Not completely." As in he hadn't consummated anything and wasn't going to admit whether he had or not. Then, despite the slight embarrassment, relief and, yes, a small dose of pride perhaps had his lips curving into a half grin. "But I have every reason to believe that *dallying* is once again a soon-to-be occurrence."

"Magnificent. That means there is hope for me yet." Warrick smiled freely and his hands maneuvered the controls so that his chair did its own little jerky dance.

Frost, aware of their difficulties, but reserved—and healthy—enough not to have been a part of their prior conversations on the topic took one stride back and coughed into his fist. "Well now. That is a most excellent development. Congratulations."

Resembling nothing so much as a Roman bust of yore, Frost had strong, blunt features further enhanced by a previously cracked nose and a decided propensity not to smile. Not to engage. Not to involve himself in extraneous goings-on, but to see to whatever duty or occurrence was happening right in front of him. Best damn officer Ed had served with, for Frost's mind was always thinking several steps ahead.

Warrick, conversely, possessed the dregs of a bankrupt title, had been planning to sell out and find a rich Diamond, exchange his title for her money. With his black hair and devil-may-care love of life and the absurd, Ed had every confidence his friend could charm his way into the dowry of any female he chose. But that was before Albuera. Before the blame battle that changed both their lives so drastically.

Now, Warrick possessed his wit, his mother's determined love, and a broken body left to woo some mushroom's daughter. And, at the moment—based on their recent conversations—minimal hope of success, but even more, absolutely no desire to try: *What marriageable female of child-bearing age would ever want to be burdened with this?* Warrick had questioned, the last time they were together, speaking softer than usual, slower than usual, his serious tone telling Ed even more than the dismissive gesture toward his groin and legs that the smiling lips and twinkling eyes hid a worried and scared man.

Ed couldn't help but glance around. Was there anyone here who might benefit his friend? A few faces looked familiar... Was that Samuel Gregory, talking to some blonde miss? Hell, he hadn't seen Sam in years. But most of the faces were foreign. Had to be friends of Mary—*Anne*—and her family.

Torn. Ed was so damn torn, he felt like a split page.

He wanted to tear off and fly up the stairs where she'd disappeared, find her and make her *listen.* Make her *explain*—

But that action would only cause more of a scandal than his tardy arrival ever could.

So he settled for Frost's typically unfriendly, vastly comforting face. "Hell, man, I cannot believe Mother managed to achieve your presence."

"Call it a miracle thanks to the Christmas

season." Said with all the droll sarcasm his friend could muster.

Ed snorted. "'Tis the season for them."

"What was that all about?" Frost gestured after the departed Mary—

Anne. Good heavens.

Ed stepped closer. Just to confirm... "Was that Miss Larchmont? Miss *Anne* Larchmont? Eldest daughter of Lord Ballenger?"

"None other." Frost grinned. "The taller, lighter-haired one, now. The darker-haired pixie with her? That is her younger sister, Miss Harriet."

"Aye, that Harriet is a pickle! Be glad 'tis the older one you're here for. Should relieve your lady wife, to know that Napoleon didn't steal all your siring abilities, I am sure," Warrick added.

"We are not married yet." *Not even close.* Ed felt the need to caution his friends as well as himself, especially after that inauspicious beginning. The one he had a desperate need to make up for. "Cannot count my chickens and all that..."

"Who needs to count chickens," Warrick said, "when there is tupping to be tallied?"

Ed had a hard time not laughing outright at the look on Frost's usually bracket-faced visage. Not above the ribald remark himself, Frost wasn't one to utter such in mixed company—unlike Warrick, who oft spoke bluntly, not above provoking his audience.

Sensing some of the worry behind the bawdy banter, Frost turned to Warrick and placed one hand on his shoulder in a comforting gesture before releasing. "And you, my friend. From my observation, nerves are among some of the last bodily tissues to heal. Give yourself more time."

"Aye. I shall continue to pray they come back to life and liven up my sorry spindle." A quick wink accompanied Warrick's outrageous words.

"Damn. It is beyond great to see you both," Ed told them. "But I do have a potential wife to woo."

"Aye. A wand to wield, you mean?" Warrick wasn't ready to let the penile-focused conversation cease, it appeared.

Ed clasped one of Warrick's hands and squeezed. "Thank—"

"Damn." Warrick flipped his grip and squeezed back. "You're stronger than you were even a week ago."

The unexpected news gave him the boost of confidence he would need in the coming hours. "Thank you for that." Ed turned to shake Frost's hand, smiling at the nod of approval when his friend tested his renewed strength for himself (Ed hadn't been above giving an extra-hearty shake). "See yourself fed and full, find a lass and entertain yourself on the dance floor"—that was directed at Frost—"or find a winsome wallflower and entertain her with your verbal flights of fancy," he told Warrick.

He took solace in the nods of encouragement each man gave him as he bowed and took his leave, both reluctantly and eagerly ready to seek out the decisively *unmerry* Anne.

"You may berate me all you wish. I shall not entertain a speck of remorse." Harriet was adamant, springing throughout the bedchamber as though her feet possessed wings. "He is to be *family* after all, Merry. My *brother. Your husband.*"

As if Anne needed reminded again.

Taking refuge after their—specifically *her*—escape up the stairs, Anne now reclined, fully clothed, upon her bed. Whilst her overly dramatic sister continued the spectacle begun at the dinner table. Only instead of complaining over dinner's disastrous goose, the mettlesome youth now waxed over their latest dinner *guest*.

The one Anne valiantly wished to put from her mind.

And how would that be possible? At his very proximity—he breathes within the walls of your home even now—are your lips not tingling? Those monstrously annoying midges in your middle not turned to wondrous waltzing nuances of want?

"Are you not relieved?" the exuberant Harri demanded, her upheld fingers counting off each benefit. "He is handsome. And pleasant. Amusing, too."

"Pfft." A hearty dose of dismay prompted the disparaging sound.

"What?" Harriet halted her dizzying skips around the room.

"Amusing?" Anne spouted incredulously. "You

think him so? After only a few seconds' acquaintance?" Because she could not deny the other two, for he was handsome. And could be pleasant. But humorous? Not a characteristic she would have attributed to him. Not now, after the deceit. *Could I make you my mistress?* The insult.

Flattering *insult. Or do you forget how very tempted you were? Have been? Curious beyond belief, as to the Warrick gamekeeper...*

"Of a certainty," her sister exclaimed, approaching the bed. "'On the battlefield, I fear.'" Harriet did a decent imitation of the bold tones they'd both just heard. "What a wit!" A girl her age should not be nearly so pithy. Or astute. Or outlandish.

The breathless abandon of skipping started once again.

Anne lifted onto one elbow to watch her energetic sister. "'Twas beyond inappropriate, Harri, for you to come out and *refer* to it."

"It?" Asked with all the false innocence of someone who belonged on the stage.

"His..." *Deformity* did not sit quite right. Neither did *disgrace*, nor *disfavor*. All words often applied to those who had suffered thus.

"Missing limb?" Harriet provided, turning serious as she jumped up on the bed and rolled to her side, propping her head on one bent arm. "'Tis a recent occurrence, is it not? His injuries? The severing of his arm?"

Mercy, spoken so very bluntly. And how was it,

after traipsing the floor for minutes, the sprite wasn't even out of breath? "Earlier this year. Why?"

"Well, it is no wonder he arrived late. And missed Sir Gala—" Said with only a single snuffle, quickly squelched. "And everything else. With him newly returned home and all, how could he be at all at ease yet—around others?

"Eating and the like. It cannot be easy, being awkward about things. And then to draw everyone's attention as well? Not only because he is returned home from war but because he is the new lord? And because you also return maimed?" Harri tapped her temple with one finger. "Why, *any* sane fellow would desire to avoid that. He deserves our compassion not your censure."

"Who says I was censorious?" *You know you were. And forget not, he's a third son, no less; ergo, not at all prepared for the responsibilities now heaped upon him.*

"Anyone within five feet of us, Merry."

Damn. Mr. Edwards' favored curse came quickly to her mind. "You are more perceptive than I wish."

Harriet just grinned. "Does that mean I can start wearing your perfume? The new sweet-water Papa brought back from London?"

"No." As Mama had told Harri time and again, she could wear scent when she turned fifteen and not a day before. "Do not lodge me in the middle, betwixt you and Mother. Besides, did not Papa gift you something as well?"

"*Pfft.* That?" Harri grimaced, and stuck her tongue out. "Some metal device meant to clean one's tongue? And with it the admonition 'You had best get to it, young lady,'" she echoed their father's sonorous tones, "'for with all the jawing you do, a plethora of dust likely resides within.' Really? One's own papa talks to them in such a manner?"

Anne chuckled. At times, 'twas easy to see where Harri came by her personality.

"Please?" her sister begged. "Just a single dab?"

"Nay. I shall not go behind Mother's back." *Except when it comes to spending the night with strangers and gamekeepers?*

"Oh, well. It was worth a try." Harriet rolled to her back and closed her eyes. "I quite like him, Anne, your Lord Redford. You will accept him, will you not?"

"I hardly know him." Lie. "*You* hardly know him." Not a lie. "How can you form an opinion as to whether you like him or not?" *And when did my fiddle-faddle-spouting little sister grow up to be so deuced clever?*

"Because he held my gaze and answered me. At the door." Her eyes blinked open and she turned her head. "I detest it when adults pretend as though I am not there or cannot hold a real thought longer than a goose."

Goose? Anne wisely refrained from addressing that.

Of a sudden, Harriet bounded from the bed and stood in front of Anne, arms akimbo, eyes alight. "He called you *Mary*. M-A-R-Y. I heard you spell the other. Why would he think that? You have met before! When?"

Caught.

"I refuse to wager with you over whist"—or anything else—"but I shall promise you a bargain. *If* you promise me something in return?"

"Go on."

Challenging opponent. Harri's forceful posture didn't ease one bit, prompting Anne to stand as well. "Allow me to speak with him tonight. Let us—Lord Redford and myself—have time and privacy between us until tomorrow."

Anne pointed one finger at Harriet's mouth. "*You* vow not to say one word—to *anyone*. And I promise to answer your questions."

"*All* of them?"

"Aye." *But that does not mean I'm bound to tell you everything.*

"How soon?"

"Tomorrow eve."

Her sister nodded. "All right. You shall have my agreement—but only if you answer *one* question now."

"*Harriet.*"

"Merry Mary Anne."

"Fine. What is it?"

"How many times has he kissed you?"

Anne sputtered. "Who says—"

"Do not try to overwit or outrage your way free. You promised."

A pox on intelligent, unrepentant younger sisters.

"Well?" Harriet spun in a circle, stopped and gave Anne an arch look. "How many?"

"Hush. I need to count."

And while Anne attempted to arrive at a number honest enough to satisfy her conscience and demure enough to salvage her pride, Harriet chortled as though Christmas had come early and late and every day in between.

10

———

SNOW KEEPER

TWO DANCES—BOTH without his participation—and one full hour later and Ed still hadn't successfully gained an audience with the recalcitrant female. As slippery as slicked soap, either she kept intentionally evading his efforts to speak with her or he was having the worst possible luck since Albuera.

She'd finally come down the stairs a short while ago but saw him waiting just outside the ballroom and darted down a corridor. She was out of sight before he'd taken three steps.

After six other females traipsed the same direction, in pairs, and back again, granting him and his friends shy glances and giggles, he'd finally deduced where his woman had likely secreted herself. And she was *his* woman; he just had to convince her of that.

Another three minutes and he was going in after her, scandal be damned.

"How long are you both staying?" he asked his friends, hoping to stave off the jingle-jangle he sensed brewing between the two men who had just joined him *outside* the, "Deuced dancing arena to avoid the chits within"—according to Frost.

"Hell, man"—from Warrick—"you talk as though the fillies in there are as terrible as combat. Go on, shake a leg with one or more."

"Not on your life."

"Which I have you to thank for, so stop wasting yours—"

"Gentlemen, no fisticuffs at my party," Ed intervened. "How long can I look forward to your charming company?" How long were the guests staying here? Tonight only? Or actually through Twelfth Night?

The long-time butler at Redford Manor, Walden, full of support over the match, treating Ed as though he was still a third son and ordering him about with, "Get thyself over to Lord Ballenger's abode with haste, my lord. Secure Miss Larchmont before the frost thaws!" But no help with details over the duration of the event.

"Charming? *Him?*" Warrick just laughed.

"Depends." Frostwood frowned, first down at Warrick, then back at Ed. "How long is this deuced party of yours supposed to last?"

"Nicholas!" Warrick chided, intentionally bumping into the other man's legs after a quick adjustment of his wheels. "Would you rush true love? Ed's happiness?"

By blazes, *Ed* was ready to rush.

Rush Anne up to the altar and into his bed.

Had her three minutes elapsed yet?

⸺⸺◆⸺⸺

"GOOD EVENING," Ed said the moment he entered the ladies' retiring room.

Two shrieks, one screech and Anne's "You cannot thrumble your way in here!" welcomed him into the feminine domain he dared breach.

"I can. For did I not just do that?"

"You make a spectacle of yourself."

"Ladies." Ignoring the woman he came to see, Ed nodded at Shrieker 1 and 2, winked toward the Lone Screecher and held the door open wide. "I appreciate your cooperation; now be gone."

"You cannot command us to leave," Anne again.

He ignored that too. "Ladies? *Out*," he barked.

"Well, I never!"

"Father will hear about this!"

Shrieker 1 and The Screecher scuttled into the hallway, complaints heavy upon their lips.

Shrieker 2 paused at the doorway to look back. "Anne, do accept him. Gallant and determined. Quite swoon-worthy, I do believe." She smiled at him. "Good luck to you, my lord."

Ed immediately renamed her Anne's Intelligent

Blonde Friend. He gave her a brief bow as she swept past him, her smile beaming.

"That was poorly done of you, Mr. Edwards. I mean *Lord Redford*." If angry eyes could spit, he'd be drenched. "Even more rude than your lateness, if possible."

He shut the door with a thump and leaned against it. "Your last little friend thought it grand. Determined *and* gallant, I am."

The room they occupied must have been decorated for its current purpose. Insipid pastels everywhere. Pink wallpaper; apricot rug. Watercolor botanical prints (more pastels) hanging in a cluster as thick as brambles.

"Pah. What does Amelia Fairfax know?" Nothing pastel about the steaming pot of ire before him, despite the pale dress and peach-colored strip of fabric or wide ribbon woven through her pulled-up hair. Her unyielding posture and hard expression showed that making things right between them would prove as difficult as he'd feared. "Today is one of the few times I have not seen her snuffling about with her nose buried in a handkerchief."

"That's a rather rude observation to make."

"Rude?" She came forward, then swung away as though repelled by his very presence. "*You* are the rude one betwixt us! What noddy-headed imbecile arrives *hours* late to a celebration held in his honor?"

Pushing off the door, he crossed the room and went after her. "Had I recalled this gathering was being held at *your* home and not Redford Manor, I would have presented myself this afternoon and well before everyone was seated for dinner."

"Stay back, Mr.—" Her arms shot out, fingers splayed, as if to fend him off. "Lord Redford! Drat you." Her harsh expression didn't ease, but her eyes glistened. With anger, still? Or mayhap something else? "Confusing tonight's destination does not explain away the last days and *weeks* you have refused to venture near."

Ah. He had his answer.

"You cannot be here," she continued. "'Tis despicable." But now he saw through the bluster.

"Yet here I remain."

"Why? 'Tis unseemly in the extreme."

She pointed to the far corner, shielded by a curtained screen. "Chamber pots reside there!" she cried. "*Three* of them"—as though that was the gravest of sins—"and one is *full*." The worst offense imaginable.

Ed laughed at her outrage. "Aromatic offal or not, I had no other choice." He stalked toward her. "You continue to avoid me."

"Not with success, it seems."

"This *is* supposed to be our betrothal ball." When she looked ready to dash off, he took one long stride and captured her hand.

"Betrothal?" She tugged. He held firm. "Yet you would rather have me as *mistress*. Or have you forgotten so very soon?"

"Nay. I may have *wanted* to offer you that position—"

"Should I be flattered?" Tugging stopped, fingers fluttered near his.

"But I did not—"

"You most certainly did!" By now, their palms had met, fingers intertwined.

"No. I specifically said *Would that I could make you my mistress.* A statement. A fact expressed. Not a question asked."

"Are you certain?" His very confidence seemed to startle her. "How can you be so positive?"

He brought the back of her hand to his lips, but her deuced glove got in the way. "For the words echoed through my garret with such frequency, such regret after you ran off that—"

"With regret?" Finally did she begin to soften. "Over what?"

"I thought never to see you again. But I hoped. Wished for the impossible."

That startled her silent, stilled her enough that he slid his hold higher and traced lazy circles over the glove.

"Lord Grayson?"

"Tucked securely in the bosom of Mother Earth." Though she didn't need to hear how the hole dug itself. "Even said a prayer to send him on his way as per your request."

"Thank you. Sincerely." When had both her hands cradled his? His truncated arm crossed in front of his chest as though reaching to join in?

Uncomfortable with the realization, he freed his

hand and started tugging off one of her gloves. "How fares the blisters?"

"Better." Once bare, he glanced at her palm to see for himself; only one jagged circle of thickened skin visible. But when he turned her palm over to bring the back of her hand to his lips, he whistled through his teeth, his thumb tracing two reddened scratches. "What happened here?"

"Harriet. And holly bushes."

Should he even ask? Before he decided, she sighed and retrieved her hand. "And yes, I wore gloves this morning. At first."

"Why were you not wearing gloves when we met?"

"My winter gloves? I took them off before digging, as I did not want to dirty them." Could one sound sheepish? "They were my favorite, fur-lined pair. Perhaps, by now home to a snug field mouse? Dragged into a rabbit warren?

"The lace half gloves beneath already relinquished to the crying toddler earlier that day, as a hopeful distraction that failed until my ticking timepiece was added."

"But what of your bonnet?" He touched her hair —and she let him.

"The wind stole my bonnet, shortly after I departed the Timmonses' carrying Lord Grayson. It could be halfway to Italy by now. My cloak? I left it with Mrs. Timmons, after seeing how pitiful her own."

"Hmm. You relinquish the cloak off your back to

help those in need. See to a lad's pet at great sacrifice to yourself. Caring and generous, it seems to me. On one hand, you would make a fine viscountess. A man could do much worse for his mate."

"And on the other? I confess curiosity over which of my faults might flow from your lips."

"On the other hand? Oh, that is all." He lifted his left arm and waved slightly crooked fingers toward her. "I only have the one to ponder with."

"You wretch, how dare you make me laugh right now."

"Anne. Anne. You realize you can give to others to your detriment, do you not?" He shook his head as though she were the most pitiful of creatures. "Two pair—gone in a week? You should marry me if for nothing more than to have a keeper. A protector, to keep you in gloves."

"A protector?"

Egad. He bent to nuzzle her cheek. "Poor choice of—"

The door burst open and he quickly straightened.

"Oh! Anne! *Finally* have I found you." The inquisitive sprite who had diverted him in the entrance hall spun wide eyes from her sister to him. "*Both* of you? In *here*? This is smashing."

Anne distanced herself from him, but not before he heard a sick moan she couldn't stifle.

"Mama and Lady Redford bid me to find each of you. Your presence—*joint* presence, they said—is required. Aye, they said that: *required*, not requested, upon the dance floor."

Ed caught Anne's dismayed gaze with his. "I thought you escorted her up to the nursery."

"So I did."

"I escaped." They paid her no mind.

Ed held out the long glove he still possessed but refused to relinquish his hold once she reached for it. "And you claim you had a hand in rearing her?"

"So I did."

"Apparently, not successfully."

"Though we all try our best..." Amusement jumped in Anne's eyes. "She tends to go her own way."

To the *rat-a-tat-tat-tat* of her slipper striking the floor, Harriet expelled a *huff*. "*She* can hear every word you are each saying."

They both ignored her.

"There are worse things in a sibling," Ed said, finally releasing his grip on the silk. "Or a child."

A CHILD?

There was that to consider, to be discussed between them. For had she not sworn to him, vehemently so, after the trying birth and disheartening day that she had no interest in ever having a child of her own?

"Adding to your kiss tally?" Harriet accused with a gleeful smile, not missing the glove exchange nor

Anne's swiftly rising blush. "I suspect what you just told me was a whisker. *Three* kisses? *Harumph.*"

"You *told* her?" Disbelief painted his tone.

"Of course not. Well, yes. No. I..." Anne floundered. How to answer when they had only, just barely, begun to speak freely with each other again?

Laughing, Harriet spoke up. "Yes, she did. That you had already met and already kissed. I remain mum tonight and tomorrow, and she answers all my questions at nightfall."

"Harriet." The groan vibrated through her chest.

"My." The deep sound surprised. It was not the sort of innocent syllable she was used to hearing from him.

"Your... *What*?" Harriet questioned brightly. "You, Lord Redford—I suppose I shan't begin calling you *brother* till after the wedding. You promised answers as well, but to prolong my good first impression, I shall endeavor to be patient."

"Will you now?" he mused, already sounding suspicious.

As well he should. "She wants something."

"I know." His astute gaze met hers, then veered toward Harri. "You will exhibit the utmost of patience in exchange for...?" he prompted.

"Next Christmas—no goose upon the table." Harriet answered so swiftly, Anne suspected she'd been waiting for the opportunity to bargain thus. "You promise no Christmas goose; I promise no patter-clatter."

"*Goose?*" His gaze bounced between hers and her sister's.

"Later," Anne assured. "I shall explain."

"Ah, *later* bodes well. All right." He turned to Harriet. "No Christmas goose served at Redford Manor for Christmas 1812. That I can promise. As to your home—"

"I shall wager with Papa."

"Very good. And, Harriet..."

"Mmm?"

"Are you able to distract our parents? The mothers, especially? Give your sister and me another... fifteen minutes?"

"Make it twenty." Anne suggested not quite ready to forgive the tardy lord as quickly as she had her gamekeeper. Not quite ready to relinquish her time with him either.

"Certainly. I excel at distractions. But not in here." Harriet grasped their hands and tugged, walking backward. "*Ladies* have matters to tend. *Private* ones. Take your bussing selves off to Papa's study—across the hall. He's in the card room with Mr. Gregory and some other fellows; your friends, I believe, Lord Redford. Be in the ballroom in just over a quarter hour, and I will pretend to search *valiantly* for you until then."

At the closed door, she paused and looked at the pair of hands she held. "Merry Anne—and you, with your glove off? *Tut-tut.*" Harri mashed their bare hands together and placed one of hers on the doorknob. "And you say you have exchanged only three kisses? Papa will ride on an elephant before I believe that!"

With a snap of skirts and a whirl of exuberance, she was gone.

"Blazes."

"Quite."

"A handful, you said?" His grip tightened upon hers. "She's a spitfire and then some."

He eased past the threshold and glanced both directions before urging Anne toward the study, but not before he turned to give her *a look*. "I hope we have ten just like her."

TEN HARRIETS?

Anne shuddered. The thought didn't bear thinking; one incorrigible, mettlesome, clever hoyden in her life was quite enough.

"And now I see exactly why Harriet sent us in here," he remarked, releasing her hand and locking the door behind them.

"As do I."

And she wasn't at all sure how she felt about it.

Not only did Papa's study enfold her within its familiar, comforting scents of leather and old books and her father's preferred flavor of snuff, but the candles were few—only a branch upon his desk and one or two in wall sconces near the door shed meager light into the cavernous room.

But it was enough to see the mistletoe hanging from a ribbon overhead.

Beside her, Mr. Ed— No, *Lord Redford* whistled, the heat of his body palpable. He indicated the vastly oversized parasite clinging from the ceiling. "I do believe that contains more berries than I have ever seen hanging from one spot, even still on the tree."

Her hand still tingled, even after being crammed back into her glove the moment he released her. Curling her fingers into a fist, she turned to him and attempted to harden her resolve. "I ask that you pull your attention from that thunderingly excessive display and let us attempt to resolve what still remains between us."

"No kisses, Mary? Damn, pardon. *Anne.* That will take some getting used to."

She placed one foot behind her and stepped backward. "For me as well."

Her attention couldn't help but be drawn to the glaring piece of vegetation. Who had Harriet convinced to hang such a heavy thing?

"If you do not want me plucking berries and stealing kisses, you best not keep drawing my awareness that direction."

The shadows deepened the intimacy breathing between them every bit as much as his husky tone. "I wish you wouldn't touch me." Why was she whispering? "It makes me want to fall into your arms, and I am not sure either of us deserve that at the moment."

"Plain speaking, indeed. That I can appreciate. For myself?" He stretched, rolled both his shoulders and lifted his hand high—it easily reached beyond the berries. Then he returned it to his side, empty. "I rather feel like celebrating. Finding you tonight was not at all what I expected."

"What did you expect?"

"Truth? Misery."

And he accused her of plain speaking?

"Here. This is for you." He riffled through his pocket and withdrew a small velvet square. "Kept it with me the last few days. On the miraculous chance I should ever cross paths with Mary again. With you."

"Not knowing where I—she—resided?"

A sharp nod confirmed the whimsy.

With fingers gone clumsy, heart pounding madly, she reached into the small velvet bag and touched something hard.

"Do you not see? You are never far from my thoughts." With care, she pulled out a small time-piece, one intended to be worn on a ribbon and still so very warm from his body. *You notice that through your gloves?*

"To replace the one you lost," he said quietly.

"I didn't lose it. I—" *Gave it away.* "Never mind." Beyond touched, she chose not to remind him of her folly.

And in defiance, stripped off her glove again to hold the token against her skin.

"I know it is nothing more than glass, gears and metal, but does this make any manner of difference whatsoever?"

Gripping the watch face near her heart, in a fist so tight the imprint of it would remain for hours, she swallowed hard. "To my desire to have your heir? Or to my desire to be your mistress?"

"To your desire to dance with me. I will accept that for now. For tonight."

"And the rest?"

"We can discuss the rest tomorrow. Next week. Next month, even. For now that I know *where* you are—*who* you are, I am determined to woo you to wife."

"You ignored me horribly. Avoided—"

"Granted, but at the time I didn't know it was *you* I was avoiding." He glanced again at the mistletoe hanging above and shifted closer to it—and to her. "To confess all, the idea of inheriting a spontaneous betrothal, along with the title and everything connected to it, directly upon losing this..." He gestured toward the overhead berries with his severed arm. "Not to mention both brothers and Father, well..."

She shoved lightly at his shoulder. "'Tis enough. More than enough. When enumerated thus, I feel a veritable shrew for the injurious feelings I fostered over your absence."

Her thumb couldn't stop its slow motion over the glass face. "This is lovely, your thoughtful gift." Her fingers below halted their similar caress of the back when thin grooves met the tips. "Wait." She held it up between them, trying to read in the dim light. "You had it engraved? What did you—"

"Mary! Blazes—*Anne*. No. Stop, will you?" He lunged for the timepiece. "I forgot—"

She raced toward the branch of candles upon Papa's desk.

They wrestled. She held firm even when his arm came round her stomach and pulled her back, her spine snug along his front. Even when he begged. "Stop. Please—"

But 'twas too late.

"I already read it."

"Damn."

Mary—
I regret not asking.
Yours, Ed

Her head jerked up and she spoke over her shoulder. "*Ed?* Your mother calls you *Ward*."

"Ed...ward. Edward Snowden Thomas Redford if you want the full introduction, discounting the title that now comes after, which I would just as soon do with you." Held indecently close, she couldn't miss his lips upon her nape... His arm nestling her closer, hand splayed as though to prevent her escape.

"Edward," she whispered. Fitting, so very fitting for her *Mr. Edwards*.

"You are not angry it's dedicated to Mary?"

"Nay, to Merry." By now, the discernible line of his erection was unmistakable between them. While he made no move to wedge it against her, neither did he make an effort to withdraw.

His scent, so clean and strong and absurdly familiar wrapped around her and she leaned into him. "Tell me true. What do you regret not asking?"

"Any number of things. Where you lived. If I could see you again." He kissed the side of her neck in between each curiosity. "If you would consider being not mistress... But mayhap more... *You*, Anne. Will you?"

Rather than flinch away, as a proper, English miss should, she wiggled ever deeper against him.

He lurched into her. "Damn. Ah, pardon."

"Will I what?" she whispered amidst more wiggling, smiling at how very much he now sounded like her unruly stranger.

"Agree to be my wife? Please?"

PLEASE.

Please?

Anne hadn't expected that.

Nay, she'd expected excuses and demands. Never anticipated a gift and an honest entreaty.

Oh please, the man may curse like a soldier but he's thoughtful—he bought you a watch—and just as intriguing and attractive as when you thought him a gamekeeper.

"I want to yell," she told him.

"At me?" he sighed, his lips leaving her neck as he straightened.

"Yes. No. I am not certain." Before he could step away, she crossed her arms over his, hugged him to her middle. Quite without intent, she squirmed back against him again. "I feel as I did with you in the snow. When we kissed. And later, by the fire... Out of breath. Determined. Frustrated. Curious and yearning. For...something."

"For *who*," he stated calmly and his spread hand swept over her abdomen once in a single stroke that stirred all manner of things to life. "For me." When she didn't respond, he continued. "Anne?"

"Aye?"

"Turn around and grant me another real kiss? Say you will be my wife. And let us tell our mothers, let them plan a wedding to do their hearts happy."

"And you?" she asked, still not turning, not looking but definitely *feeling*—that hard ridge so firm along her flesh. "Will your heart be happy? Or only pacified until another cat-burying, babe-mourning, would-be mistress stumbles across your path?"

"Anne," he groaned, whipping her around to face him so fast she yelped. "Scream if you must—any number of truly gallant men shall race to your rescue. But if a man—me—has both wife and mistress in one, how could he ever think to look for another?"

"I..."

While she stood there within his embrace, staring into earnest eyes so blue they stole her breath, her very speech, he swore. "Pardon. Anne, if it takes months, I want to make our betrothal real."

Which started to allay her hesitation—until he

spoke again. "I want you for my wife. I want *you* to mother my children."

"You rush ahead of yourself." *Of me.*

"I care naught. I want—"

"*Merrrrow.*"

Anne looked down. Beatrice didn't just announce her presence, approach and weave her willowy length around his ankles—though she did, twice.

Nay, Anne's normally distant feline *launched* herself straight up his pantaloons, his through-the-teeth hiss unmistakable when her claws gouged through fabric and skin.

But instead of shouting *Damn cat!* and kicking her off, he scooped up and cradled Beatrice as though she were precious. His hand supporting her hindquarters, her head and front paws resting in the crook of his elbow as he kept her tucked against his chest, his truncated arm resting lightly on her side. "Hello, sweetheart. And who might you be?"

Anne's heart cracked wide. "But you don't like cats."

"You are wrong there." She watched his strong fingers thread back and forth through Beatrice's white and grey fur, the simple action keeping her in thrall. Her and her usually timid cat both. "Always have I held felines with affection. Ever since a prolific family of mice invaded my bedchamber when I was a lad and left undesired doodles every-where, and Mr. Cheese Pot came to the rescue."

"*Cheese Pot?*"

She laughed until she choked. Laughed again, and then came to her senses when she realized how loudly her sweet kitty was purring.

"This is Beatrice." Anne scratched the short fur between the cat's ears, delighted when Beatrice closed her eyes and purred even louder.

"Beatrice? Like her mama, then? *And a good soldier to a lady, but what is she to a lord?*"

"Did you just misquote Shakespeare at me?"

"I did indeed."

He thought she and her cat favored the spirited heroine in *Much Ado About Nothing*?

"Neither of us are anything like her," Anne answered. "I'm surprised you would think so. To hear Mother speak of it, I am rather complacent, if truth be told."

He barked a laugh. "You? *Complacent?* Not hardly. Not the argumentative female I have known since she tore into my hide during a blizzard."

She was the calmest one in her family. Always had been. Against Mother's hysterics over Harriet's constant foibles, Harriet herself, not to mention Papa indulging her whims, Anne had always considered herself... Well, the boring, tepid Larchmont. "I believe you are mistaken."

"And you suffer delusions." He shifted as Beatrice tried to turn around upon her one-armed perch. "So tell me of your Bea... When she isn't mutilating houseguests and their attire, how does she please herself?"

"Mostly by hiding under furniture unless she's

chasing dinner. Much like your Mr. Cheese Pot, she rather fancies mice but prefers grasshoppers. Expect to find them in your bed, sometimes still alive."

"My bed?" He eyed her from beneath raised brows, now stroking the underside of Bea's chin as the cat had climbed up his chest and wound herself around his shoulders, to Anne's wonderment. "Or yours?"

"For shame." She might have protested, but she fairly glowed inside. *He liked cats. He thought her lively.*

And argumentative, lest you become complacent and forget—

She shook off the marvel of the past few seconds. "*That* sort of talk I shall invite after more kisses and more time."

"And I shall be delighted to give you both."

11

SNOW'S BLISS

———◦◦———

THE BEING who had no right to read the letter now within his possession, nevertheless opened the folded square with great care, smoothed the creases and read the words he'd practically committed to memory in just a short few days. Proof that his idea pot wasn't totally betwattled, eh?

Ward,
Your father has not worn this for ages. It no longer fits his podgy finger.

You need not fear the taint of his soul upon it, for I have cleansed it every way I could conceive before bringing it to you. It has been washed with water, with soap (two types), even with salt water. After praying over it, I laid it out along my window ledge during the day and let the sun burn any residual ill will and all hints of the man who wore this before you. (I left it on the ledge during two full moons as well, so the fairies could lend their aid, but let us not speak of that again, lest you think to commit me to Bedlam.)

No matter how many times he read it, that always managed to bring a rare and rusty chuckle to the surface.

As is beyond apparent, I have done everything I could think of to bring this symbol of our family back to the neutral state it should be in before you, my dear Ward, place it upon your finger and wear it with the respect and honor it deserves.

Your father and brothers may have done all they could to besmirch our family name, but I have no doubt you will find a way to return it to the prestige that is its right.

"Poor cuss."

Phineas remarked upon the unknown fellow whose family Bible contained a wealth of worn pages but no discernible name of its owner. Smaller than many, likely meant for travel and not recording ancestors.

"Heavy weight she's tasked you with, my unknown, one-handed friend, this fond mother of yours."

How I wish I could recall mine.

———————◆———————

He liked cats.

No matter how many times she acknowledged the truth of it, the realization warmed her down to her slippered toes.

They had arrived, as *required*, at the ballroom only to find a frolicking reel just underway. A shared look confirmed they were in accord—neither wishing to traipse upon the dance floor, scuttling others out of their way to claim their place.

When Lady Redford bustled over, Anne encouraged Ed to enjoy a private moment with his mother.

So here she stood, off to the side. hoping not to elicit Mama's attention quite yet. Hoping no one else noticed her either, came to gabber and begged the next dance. For her spiraling thoughts would no doubt twist her feet and land her in a heap.

As if your reckless actions of a few days prior haven't already done so!

He liked cats...

Surely you will accept him now?

A bracing breath inhaled the scents of fresh greenery and spiced wassail set out for the season, while she tried not to notice how many sprigs of mistletoe, bound and tied with ribbons, her sister had managed to procure.

If you don't, he will no doubt pursue someone else. Must get an heir, that is his duty above all else now.

The thought of this man, *her* Mr. Edwards, Lord Redford, Ward...*Ed*, with another woman at his side pierced her heart like a dagger. Had she not acted the scold toward Amelia Fairfax if for no other reason than the pleasant young woman had dared to smile at him, to speak in favor of him?

"Merry Anne?" He'd returned!

Yet his unusually somber tone caused no little amount of angst. "Aye, Lord Redford?"

"I seem to have found myself in quite the quandary. Might I beg your counsel with regards on the best way to move beyond my currently mired state?"

"But of course."

"You see, Miss Larchmont, I am confounded by a situation I find myself in."

Dash it! He'd been speaking with his mother. What if, after the contretemps when he arrived, Lady Redford had taken a dislike—

Do not worry about things not yet expressed.

But worry she did, all the more, the more he scowled.

"If you have no desire to further our acquaintance because of how Harriet—or I—behaved, could you not simply state it outright? Why make me suffer through a dance—"

"Suffer? Is that what a turn with me would be?"

"If you only seek to do so in order to sever any future interaction, then aye." What had her in such a ruffle? "Cruel indeed."

"And if I seek to *further* our association?"

"Then why the devil not just blasted *ask* me?" She indicated the throng now bowing and curtsying as the song came to an end. "Did your mother say something?"

"Mother? Whatever do you mean?"

"Why cause me no small amount of angst?"

"Anne." He gripped her flailing arm, tightened his fingers around her wrist till the pressure stifled her words. "You gravely misunderstand. I want nothing more than to contemplate a union between us, but—damn it, woman—I claim no inkling of how the devil to *dance*"—just then, as though to vex him beyond measure, the musicians began a vivacious waltz—"much less *waltz* with you when I have no notion of what to do with *this*."

He waved the shortened arm, covered in his best tailcoat, quickly folded and sewn that afternoon when he'd gone by Redford Manor, thinking that his destination for the party. "How in blazes do I complete the steps? Clasp your hand with *this*?"

"Oh, for goodness' sake. Is *that* truly what has been bothering you? I thought you were about to cry off."

"What gave you that notion? And you call *me* a noddy-head?"

Capable Anne took charge, the one who had so impressed him on the Spierton grounds; wrapping one arm around the side of his waist and tugged him toward her, her other hand—the one in an ideal world he would be grasping overhead with his, she slid just beneath his arm, bringing hers up until his shortened appendage rested gently along it. "Like this, you imbecile."

No matter that it should have been the opposite, missing one, he braced his hand firmly against the middle of her back and found that guiding her where he wanted them to go was a relatively simple matter of exerting the lightest amount of pressure. She followed him wonderfully.

The memory of learning the dance—all the various parts of it—thanks to Warrick one drunken night in Portugal, threatened to addle him. Warrick, the most accomplished dancer among them, who could no longer walk, much less aspire to *dance...*

But on the next spin, a glance toward the French windows showed his seated friend near one, engaged in an animated conversation with Anne's Intelligent Friend as frowning Frost looked on, which kept the sorrow at bay. Most of it, at least. For they had all three made it home, not something he could say for everyone who had reveled that fun and boozy night.

When the tempo changed, alerting them to assume the next hold as they added a hop to their spinning steps, the transition went smoother than he'd feared. Both her hands now firmly curved over his shoulders. And though both of his should have been upon either side of her waist, he gripped her warm flesh with only his left hand and simply brought his shortened arm up beneath hers.

She nodded her approval, eyes brimming with joy, as they hopped and spun, circling the dance floor along with every other pair daring enough to join in.

Staring into Anne's face, memorizing every imperfect, alluring feature, every exquisite inch that beckoned him to kiss and touch and look a thousand years more, brought the fiercest sense of rightness he had known in years.

"Last time I did this—hell, the only time—beg pardon, I partnered Warrick and we were both so cupshot we were seeing double." After several jaunty turns, holding her gaze all the while, he was finally able to relax sufficiently to savor partnering her. "Not sure I realized how much better this would be with someone other than a bosky soldier. With you." His fingers flexed against her waist. "How close we would be."

"I know. It's practically indecent," she said smugly. "I quite like it."

"I quite...like you." The exertion filched his breath.

"Even when I am foolish?"

He swung her around in an exhilarating turn, one that lifted his feet—along with his heart.

The music changed yet again, each pair expected to add a skip-hop, a little kick, to the already brisk effort. "You, my dear, are never foolish. Though on occasion...I admit you might attempt foolish things."

"Hurrumph."

Another vigorous turn and his knee buckled, leg crumpled, hurtled them both toward the floor.

His arms released her and wheeled about. His feet stuttered but couldn't keep up.

Down he went, his knee heading toward a burning collision with—

But nay.

Anne was there.

To the—imagined?—collective gasp of their audience?

But there nevertheless, her stalwart shoulder and self, the woman who had birthed babes and buried cats in the biting wind (or nearly so)—there to land her strength and support as she lurched and ducked beneath him. Saving both his knee and his pride.

The periphery of the ballroom—even the other dancers themselves—ceased to matter as she straightened, her shoulder wedged beneath his, her arms hugged around his middle every bit as tight as they'd been when they said *goodbye* scant days prior.

"Dear Anne..." His breath still faltered, the near calamity a mental fright as much as a physical one. "You lend me strength and balance."

"'Tis a fortunate thing, my lord, for your dancing is just pitiful."

He laughed. *Laughed* at the weakened leg that hadn't—thanks to her—mortified him beyond reckoning, but had only annoyed. For the first time since falling on that soggy battlefield, he was almost thankful for it, for had he kept his seat on the borrowed horse, they would have missed out on those magical stolen hours together.

The musicians had jangled to a discordant stop, silent for a handful of seconds, then they resumed their original, slower melody, the one that signaled the dancers to turn and spin—but not jump or skip, thank heavens.

"Shall we stop?" she asked, looking as anxious as his mother and as concerned as Anne's father, both hovering on the outskirts of the dance floor, poised as though to rush to his aid. He jerked a quick nod, acknowledging them, hoping he conveyed the steadiness with which he now commanded both his feet and the moment. Then he turned back to Anne.

"Absolutely not." He lifted his hand over her head. "This is still our dance, I believe?"

With a grin, she gripped him once more and they were off, her very presence subduing the ache in his leg.

"You 'my lorded' me earlier. There is no need. Call me Ed. It's what my friends use. *Lord Redford* is far too staunch and pompous for two souls as akin as I think we may be."

She gave their joined hands a squeeze. "And you may call me Merry."

"Might you, perhaps... Merry Anne," he broached as tactfully as he could think to, "reconsider your stance against birthing a babe?"

Heat flared over her pretty face, flushing cheeks and brightening eyes. Her fingers upon his back stiffened. "Have you knowledge of something I do not?"

"Only that an heir would delight my mother

even more than if we—you and I—were to make an announcement tonight."

"Hmm. An announcement, you say?"

"Mmm. Something similar to *I declare, I do hope we have something other than goose for Twelfth Night.*"

"You can be a cork-brained idiot."

"Aye. Would you have me any other way?"

"I begin to think I shall have you just as you are." She released his hand to run the tips of her fingers over the hastily sewn tailcoat seam, warming scarred flesh he'd wished dead during the worst of his recovery.

"This has never bothered you, has it? Not once have you expressed any manner of hesitation over my deformity."

"A deformity it is not," she stated with assurance. "It would have to *be there* to be deformed."

Damned if he didn't laugh again. "And that is why I want you for my wife. You may be stubborn; I *know* you are. And argumentative— Nay. Do not interrupt me here. We—"

Yet again the music changed; yet again, the musicians kept it spry but unhurried. He and Anne lowered their arms, still holding onto each other, still staring only at each other. "Yes, argumentative. We can argue over that one later, if you wish. For you are also caring and forthright and bring me such unexpected delight. You are all I never thought to wish for and you are here, in my arms, and I vow, I do not want to let you go." *Arms?* "Arm. Damn it."

"Hush. Corrections or admonitions such as that between us never need be uttered."

But what did need uttered...

"Your heated proclamation about the messy, disgusting business of birthing a child, about not begetting any of your own... Is that something you might reconsider? Or were you in earnest?"

"I was hungry, cold, exhausted, and sad. Aye, I meant every word."

"Oh."

"Then." Confusion trenched his brow. "I meant the words *then*," she said. "Now? Can it be too soon for me to claim a change of heart?"

His fingers tightened just above her hip. "Hearing that makes me the most blissful of fellows. I want nothing more than to dance you right out the nearest French window and sweep you out into the garden where I might have you all to myself."

She looked that direction. Dare he hope—with longing? "It is rather cold outside."

"I daresay that I could keep you warm."

Eyes glittering, she pulled her hand from his shoulder and fanned her face. "I am feeling significantly warm, if not overly flushed right now."

"It has been a lengthy waltz."

"Quite. I wonder why the musicians haven't halted before now."

"Because each time your mother or mine caught my eye and pointed to the gallery, I indicated they should keep playing."

"Are you attempting to make a point, Lord Redford?"

"I am attempting to gain a wife."

That confident, bold statement begat a herd of butterflies in Anne's stomach, ones that quite outfluttered the midges. "And a babe in the bargain?"

"In due time. There exists no immediate race to that end. Although I shall enjoy the begetting of one, I am sure, and would endeavor that you do the same."

She snickered. Could not help herself. "Ensure *you* enjoy the begetting?"

"No, you vexatious piece of baggage, ensuring that you do."

"Did you not prove that the other night?"

The tips of his ears grew red. "I, ah, was not at my best that night. I am firmly of the opinion you would benefit... Appreciate... Find me more impressive, and yourself more pleasure, should we repeat the experience."

Anne gave a gasp of mock outrage. "Why, Lord Redford, you outlandish fiend! Are you seeking to see me ruined?"

"Only if you refuse to have me any other way."

Did he but know it, every second spent in his company was one closer to her not only acceding to the betrothal, but embracing it with all her might.

"I do not know," she pondered, glancing up at the ceiling in a bored fashion. "What, exactly, do you have to recommend yourself? Nay—hush now," she ordered when he started to speak. "It is my turn to enumerate your qualities. Be they positive or negative."

"Go on. I await your every declaration with breath held and the rest of me a bag of nails."

"You do know how to make a roaring fire."

"One that doesn't last."

"And you are rather handy with a shovel."

He snorted a laugh. "And you have a monstrous sense of humor."

She gave him a nod of agreement, and couldn't stop the grin that threatened. "I did enjoy your kisses, what I have sampled of them so far."

"Ah, yes. My kisses are quite acclaimed."

"Let us keep them betwixt ourselves henceforth. No *mistressing* about." His eyes glittered but he remained silent. "You rake. That was an opportunity for you to agree."

"Mmm. My remarkable qualities, you were saying?"

Stifling laughter, she admitted, "I do so adore your mother"—especially knowing that Lady Redford hadn't tried to dissuade their union—"especially how she—"

"Mother? What has she to do with *us*?" His chin thrust out toward her, encompassed himself and the entire gathering. "Except, of course, helping to arrange *all* of this."

"A tremendous amount, actually. If she had not convinced me of your worth, if I did not count her as a friend, we would not be here now. Together."

"My worth? She did not attempt to use sympathy to gain your patience?"

"Not one bit. Only cited your affable, caring personality, at complete odds with the other males in her household."

Astonishment widened his eyes. "So she did not tell you of the broken leg and crushed hand? Of this?" He raised his truncated arm.

"None of it. She only mentioned—once, mind—that you had suffered an injury and were expected to heal."

"Had she," he said slowly, "told you the full truth, you would have known who I was that night."

"But would we not have been cautious with each other, had we known? Remote from the very beginning? I, for one, was much more at ease with my simple soldier than I would have been had I known who you were from the onset."

"Can you imagine," he posed, "if we had known? Our conversation would have been dreadfully dull."

"Disappointingly droll."

"Terribly tepid."

He stopped dancing and hugged her, right there on the ballroom floor, in sight of every guest and all three parents. "I never thought to bandy words with a wife as I have my friends. I would count myself the most fortunate of men to have found both: wife and friend."

"What about mistress?" she asked archly.

"Anne, I think our bed will already be full enough without adding anyone else."

After the energetic waltz that lasted far longer than intended, the musicians took a well-deserved rest, leaving their instruments in the gallery and stepping away.

Something Ed was ferociously thankful for, as the turning and twisting had wrangled up his leg until the bones and surrounding flesh were screaming at him. Yelling louder than he'd ever thought to howl.

He couldn't help but admire how, with a sharp shake of her head, Anne warned off their mothers as the pair scuttled over, pointedly sent them scurrying the other way.

"Well done, my dear." He hoped she didn't hear the groan as his body protested each step.

"We both know they want us to stand up and announce *something other than* your Twelfth Night goose nonsense, but if you don't sit and rest, I'm afraid you shall land upon your nose, rendering it as crooked as Lord Frostwood's."

At that astute observation, he realized he had gripped her shoulder and was leaning on her heavily as they left the dance floor. She found the nearest two empty chairs and ordered, "Wait here. I shall return."

Then she swept off in a whirl of command and the lightest hint of some flowery fragrance he had every intention of whiffing out where she'd applied it the moment he could get her alone.

For now, the screaming ache made him doubly thankful for her capable manner—even if he wasn't used to being on the receiving end of orders from anyone but his superior officer.

She joined him a minute later, handing him a glass. "Father's brandy, smuggled from his study," she said with a smile. "Of a higher quality than what he allowed Mother to serve everyone else."

Seating herself next to him, it was a pleasant two or three swallows later when he realized it was probably the longest they had jointly gone without speaking. Simply watching the crowd, watching her wave away anyone who dared approach, brought him a measure of peace he wasn't sure he'd ever known.

In silence, he finished his drink and bent to place the empty glass beneath his chair. As he straightened, pushing his feet into the floor to give him leverage, his teeth clenched on a light moan.

"Thank you, Anne. I admit I lingered overly long out there and, in all honesty, shouldn't dance again this evening."

"Of course not. Do you think I didn't notice how pronounced your limp just now? We must take care not to overdo in the future."

He took heart from that *we*. "Ah, I have every expectation that my leg will heal fully, or close to it, in time. But, ah, none that the rest of my arm will reappear."

"*Ah*, is right." Holding a glass of wassail, wafting cloves and other spices, in one gloved hand, she placed her other upon his and gave a gentle squeeze. "Fingers and forearms tend not to be like hair and nails."

"Fingernails. Missing five of those too, I fear."

"Your sense of the absurd seems adequately intact."

"Only adequately? I am wounded." She left off watching the dancers and angled toward him. Her eyes drifted over his chest and shoulders, past his hips and legs, down to his feet before she lifted her gaze to his.

Hazel heated, her grey-green irises flaming with an inner fire he'd not seen from her before. "Nay. No longer wounded, my lord. I do believe you healed."

Her words, her acceptance of all he was—and wasn't—lifted his cheeks in a soft smile.

"Will you..." Her words so quiet, he had to lean forward to hear. "Will you tell me what happened?" Her meaning clear as crystal when she wrapped her fingers around the flesh above his cut bone wiping the contented smile free.

"Now?" It was a croak.

Because he knew she wasn't asking for the flippant responses he might give Harriet.

Nothing so trivial for his merry Anne. Nay, she would require he bare his pain, his fears, his very soul, to tell her without demure all that had happened that tragic day—and afterward.

"Only when you're ready to speak of it. Not before."

"Then yes," he told her, the truth of it sighing from deep within his chest. "I will."

"I will as well."

"Will what?"

"Don't be obtuse." She toasted him with her glass. "Marry you, you imbecile."

"Really, my dear, your propensity to utter insults is one thing between us. But definitely not something I shall tolerate among others."

Had he overstepped?

Apparently not, for instead of looking intimidated—or respectful, which is what he had been hoping for—she just laughed and took another sip.

EPILOGUE

———◦———

THE FOLLOWING AUTUMN, 1812

"MY LADY?" Walden, the butler at Redford Manor, scratched upon the open door to the sitting room where Anne was composing a letter to Isabella. This after the missive in response to Harriet's complaints of *everlasting tedium* had been finished and folded.

Walden, whom she'd learned was the older brother of Wilson, who occupied the same position at the Larchmont abode.

"Different mothers," Wilson had explained that long-ago morning after the betrothal announcement, when he'd been up early, overseeing the staff as they righted things from the party the night before, and she was just seeking her bed after hours with Ed and the wonder that she'd agreed to marry him.

"Wilson, you welcomed Lord Redford with ease," she'd said, "mentioned seeing him *again*. You have met?"

"Not only met, known the rapscallion since he was a lad. My half brother, Walden, he's been their butler since well before Miss Harriet joined the family and started livening things up."

Same pater, different mothers; which is why she hadn't noticed a resemblance between the two men. But also explained why Wilson knew her betrothed, as his brother had known the Redford men for years and, like Ed's mother, had a particular favorite.

"Yes, Walden?" She tucked a stubborn strand of hair behind her ear. "Come to issue complaint about the housekeeper again?" A woman he was sweet on —sparking behind their backs, if she read things correctly—but made it a point to bluster about as though the competent female had no idea how to direct maids in the polishing of silver nor the dusting of frivolities. "Has she once again failed in her airing of the linens?"

He coughed into his gloved fist, eyes alight. "Not this time, my lady. I do believe there is a carriage whisking down the drive you might have a keen interest in."

"Visitors?" She sprung from her chair, barely grappling the pen back into its holder, and not without ink splotching the unfinished letter.

Ed had left for London the morning prior, and the house had been dreadfully quiet without his amusing, irritating presence. "Whoever might it be?"

They hadn't been married overly long, and no one had written ahead to announce their arrival.

When she reached the front door, opened wide by a smiling Walden, one footman hovering just behind—at least with the decency to bite his grin—Anne raced to look out the door, only to falter to a surprised halt.

Ed?

'Twas his carriage that flew down the drive.

His voice that bid their coachman take the carriage back to the mews.

His strong body that jumped to the ground before the steps were down, his bright eyes that shone like the deepest blue of a hot flame as his powerful legs devoured the distance between them, took the stairs two at a time, and presented his unexpected carcass directly before her.

"You are home a week early!" Not that she minded, for the exuberant, hearty hug he gave her had the servants melting into the background and her body doing the same—melting in readiness for this most excellent of men. "What a delight! But why?"

He'd gone to London—or so she thought—to look at three different townhouses his man of affairs had found, planning to choose one to rent or buy before the upcoming parliamentary sessions, his first as a peer (the prior year not one to count, given all he'd endured).

"Even one night away proved misery." Ed leaned back and loosened his arms, raising his hand to brush back that loose fall of hair. "And I was to endure several more? Nay, either you come with me or we find someone else to inherit. This parliamentary minutia is not for me."

Not the first time he'd rattled on about a lack of interest in taking his place alongside a bunch of other "pompous bastards, pardon", stuffed into the city like "rats on a barge".

"Ah. Dear Mr. Edwards," she rose up on her toes to whisper in his ear—something she only called him when no one else could hear. "Do you need to start training horses in London? Would that help?"

"Impracticable. But having you there might."

"If that is what you wish. I know Father always used the time away to visit the hells, do some gambling, coze with his cronies."

"You have met my two cronies. I doubt any of us are bound for the hells. Warrick's still attached to wheels. Frost in the thick of wavering between caring for his estates while avoiding his mother. I've never met the woman, but gather she goes out of her way to be a maggoty trial.

"Me? I want to be in the thick of you. Damn me. Didn't come out right. Pardon."

By now, more than familiar with the informal way he expressed himself when they were alone, she just smiled and adjusted a fold in his neckcloth. "I think you express yourself just fine."

"Speaking of, I stopped at Warrick's, to visit with him for the night."

"Wonderful. I was hoping you might."

"Have you a friend perhaps, for Warrick? Someone we could introduce him to? She only need have loads of blunt, no keen interest in having any children, and not mind if he cannot take her dancing. In other words, someone exceedingly kind and exceptionally desperate..." By the time he finished, Ed looked as though he'd sucked a lemon: face puckered, nose crinkled, the hearty sigh that followed the improbable list admitting defeat before she had a chance to respond. "Let us pretend the topic as buried as Owen's cat, shall we?"

She swatted his shoulder for that. "No one comes readily to mind, but give me time to consider. Your other friend now? Frowning Frostwood?"

He chuckled. "Do not let him hear you say that."

"For your ears only." She rose to her toes and kissed just below one of his. "After you left, I received another chatty letter from Harriet. She claims she has found him the perfect match."

"Ah... Lord Redford?" Walden stepped forth. "My lady? Please forgive the interruption. I do believe we have more guests."

A startled glance out the door they hadn't moved away from sufficiently for anyone to shut, showed a couple approaching up the drive. The man—equipt to the nines, from his tall topper to his polished if out-of-fashion heeled shoes, well-fitted burgundy tailcoat, dark blue breeches and pale silk stockings in between—was absurdly dressed for daytime. But presented a bang-up figure indeed.

Conversely, his companion wore a light blue day

dress beneath a simple cloak. The most smashing bonnet Anne had ever seen covered a shock of outrageously orange hair.

"Do you know him?" Anne asked, spying his white-knuckled grip clutched about a tied parcel as he strode up the drive, his companion's gloved hand resting upon his opposite forearm, his fist clenched just as tight.

"Nay." Ed tugged Anne in front of him, kept hold of her hand and whispered, "Remain by my side. Murmurings heard of late allude to nefarious goings-on in the area."

Murmurings? *Nefarious?* She'd demand details later, when they were alone.

The man practically marched toward the door, a scowl upon his countenance that quite reminded her of Lord Frostwood, although this fellow was a stranger to her. His companion let her hand drift off his arm and paused several paces from the steps that he climbed; eleven, Anne knew, already having made note of every staircase in the large abode, hopeful for the time Isabella might be permitted to visit.

He came straight up to the third tread and halted.

"Greetings." His voice, all deep gravel and hard edges, filled the empty, curious space between them.

Safety assured by the powerful man at her back, Anne assumed her duties as Lady of the Manor, the Dowager Redford now not only inhabiting the dower house, but at the moment away visiting a friend near Brighton. "You have reached Redford Manor. Is that your destination?"

The bang-up stranger with glittering eyes and a forceful demeanor one could sense a mile away glanced over his shoulder, toward the female who had accompanied him.

She aimed a bright, encouraging smile his way.

At her nod, he turned back to them and tilted his head in a bow. He brought the parcel up from his side. "Sincerest apologies." The man swallowed as though scraping that much out was a chore. "Lord Redford?"

"Aye?"

"These belong to you, I believe." His gaze fell to Ed's missing hand. He nodded once. "Aye. They do."

The moment Ed shuffled her behind him to take the proffered package, the other man spun on his heel and bounded down the stairs in a single jump. All eight of them? Anne shivered; had she seen that right?

Two more steps and he captured the hand of the woman waiting a few yards back and they disappeared into the trees part way down the long drive.

"That was peculiar." Anne left off staring where the couple had vanished to pluck at the string secured round the parcel. "Have you any notion of what's inside?"

But Ed was still staring after the stranger, down the now-empty drive, a thoughtful expression settling a curious frown between his brows. "Did you see his feet? I do believe that fellow is wearing my shoes."

THE END

Note from Larissa

Howdy! Still craving more Regency Christmas? Read Isabella and Lord Frostwood's story in *A Frosty Christmas Kiss*, a Gayle Wilson Award of Excellence finalist.

For more about Phineas, their four-footed matchmaker, and my steamy Regency Shifters, check out the first Roaring Rogues book, Maggie Award of Excellence finalist, *Ensnared by Innocence*.

Thanks for reading!

>^..^< Larissa Lyons

ABOUT LARISSA

HUMOR. HEARTFELT EMOTION. & HUNKS.

A lifelong Texan, Larissa writes steamy regencies, blending heartfelt emotion with doses of laugh-out-loud humor. Her heroes are strong men with a weakness for the right woman.

Avoiding housework one word at a time (thanks in part to her super-helpful herd of cats >^..^<), Larissa adores brownies, James Bond, and her husband. She's been a clown, a tax analyst, and a pig castrator(!) but nothing satisfies quite like seeing the entertaining voices in her head come to life on the page.

Writing around some health challenges and computer limitations, it's a while between releases, but stick with her...she's working on the next one.

Learn more at LarissaLyons.com.

amazon.com/author/larissalyons
bookbub.com/authors/larissa-lyons
goodreads.com/larissalyons
facebook.com/AuthorLarissaLyons
instagram.com/larissa_lyons_author

Ensnared by Innocence
STEAMY REGENCY SHAPESHIFTER

2022 Maggie Award of Excellence Finalist

Changing into a lion isn't all fur and games.

A Regency lord battles his inner beast while helping an innocent miss, never dreaming how he'll come to care for the chit—nor how being near his world will deliver danger right to her doorstep.

If Darcy had been a shape-shifting lion who thought about frisking—a lot...

STANDALONE ~ HEA ~ 80,000-WORD NOVEL ~ BOOK 1 - ROARING ROGUES REGENCY SHIFTERS

Note: This love story between two people contains some profanity and a lot of sizzle, including one partial ménage scene that gets rather...growly.

Deceived by Desire
STEAMY REGENCY SHAPESHIFTER

Meet a Shakespeare-quoting shapeshifter who wants nothing to do with love...

Cursed into the form of a lion without nightly sex, Lord Nash Hammond wants only two things—his liquor strong and smooth, and his wenches wild and willing. What he doesn't need is a virgin!

HEA ~ BOOK 2 – ROARING ROGUES REGENCY SHIFTERS ~ 97,000 WORDS

*Reader Advisory: While Deceived by Desire is laugh-out-loud funny in places, it contains a short *vision* of violence and brief references to past abuse. Beyond that, expect a fun and sexy good time because...*

Changing into a lion is all fun and growls—until it isn't.

Mistress in the Making Trilogy

A fun, emotionally satisfying, steamy tale told in three parts: Seductive Silence, Lusty Letters, and Daring Declarations.

Seductive Silence, Part 1
FREE at all retailers

Lord Tremayne has a problem. He stammers like a fool—at least that's what he learned from his father's constant criticism and punishing hand. Daniel now hides his troubles by barley saying anything. But then he goes looking for a new mistress and finds a delightful young woman who makes him, of all people, want to spout poetry. He thought he had a problem before? Avoiding meaningless dinner prattle is nothing compared to the challenge of winning the heart of his new lady lust.

Lusty Letters, Part 2

Thea's fascinating new protector has secrets—several. Hesitant to destroy her newfound circumstances, she stifles her longing to know everything about the powerfully built—and frustratingly quiet—Marquis. But then his naughty notes start to appear, full of humor and wit, and Thea realizes she's about to break the cardinal rule of mistressing —that of falling for her new protector. *Egad.*

Daring Declarations, Part 3

An evening at the opera could prove Lord Tremayne's undoing when he and his lovely new paramour cross paths with his sister and brother-in-law. Introducing one's socially unacceptable strumpet to his stunned family is *never* done. But Daniel does it anyway. And it might just be the best decision he's ever made, for Thea's quickly become much more than a mistress—and it's time he told her so.

Lady Scandal

Sparks—and stockings—fly when an interview for a husband turns into a game of forfeits—played with articles of clothing—a scandalous lady and one handsome rogue learn how very right for each other they are.

Lady Scandal **awarded the Golden Nib!** "I can't praise this book enough. Regency fans, if you like gorgeous wit in with your devilishly superb, well written, sexy reading matter, Lady Scandal should be on your 'Must Read' list." *Natalie, Miz Love & Crew Love's Books*

Top Pick from ARe Café: "[Lady Scandal] is the most flirtatious, sensual, and delectable treat." *Lady Rhyleigh, ARe Café* ~ Selected as a **Recommended Read!**

LARISSA'S COMPLETE BOOKLIST

Historicals by Larissa Lyons

ROARING ROGUES REGENCY SHIFTERS

Ensnared by Innocence

Deceived by Desire

Tamed by Temptation (TBA)

REGENCY CHRISTMAS KISSES

A Snowlit Christmas Kiss

*A Frosty Christmas Kiss**

A Moonlit Christmas Kiss (TBA)

*(formerly *Miss Isabella Thaws a Frosty Lord*)

MISTRESS IN THE MAKING series (Complete)

Seductive Silence

Lusty Letters

Daring Declarations

Mistress in the Making - Bundle

FUN & SEXY REGENCY ROMANCE

Lady Scandal

Contemporaries by Larissa Lynx

SEXY CONTEMPORARY ROMANCE

Renegade Kisses

Starlight Seduction

SHORT 'N' SUPER STEAMY

A Heart for Adam...& Rick!

Braving Donovan's

No Guts, No 'Gasms

POWER PLAYERS HOCKEY series

*My Two-Stud Stand**

*Her Three Studs**

The Stud Takes a Stand (TBA)

**Her Hockey Studs - print version*